Hearts Reawakened

Echoes of Camano Island

Kimberly Thomas

Prologue

The warm June air filled Trish's lungs as she stepped onto the porch of her cozy home. The sun hung low in the sky, casting a gentle golden hue over the verdant landscape and the far-off peaks of the majestic Olympic Mountains. Towering evergreens blocked her view of the endless expanse of the ocean, but sporadic flashes of the glittering Saratoga Passage winked at her, and the subtle tang of salt was carried on the swirling wind. The scene was nothing short of a masterpiece.

Nestling into the familiar embrace of her wicker chair, she unfurled her legs in a languid stretch, releasing a sigh of contentment. Her eyes drifted shut.

"I thought I'd find you here."

The unexpected voice startled her into alertness, and her eyes flew open to see Paul, her friend and business partner, climbing the porch steps. Trish hastily rearranged her posture as he came to a halt before her. A

1

friendly smile brightened his face, and his green eyes twinkled.

"Hi." Trish returned the smile. "I wasn't expecting you today. Is everything okay?" she asked.

"Yeah. Everything's... great," he replied, his reassurance lacking conviction. "You don't have to get up." He halted her mid-movement.

Trish, poised halfway in her ascent, melted back into the familiar comfort of the chair.

"I just came by to see how things were going at the restaurant, seeing that I now have a lot of free time on my hands." Even though his tone was light, Trish sensed the underlying tension.

"I know it's not easy having to take a step back from the day-to-day operations at Lot 28, but it's necessary if it means that it will keep you healthy," she spoke encouragingly.

Paul gave a short laugh. "Easier said than done." His fingers combed through his dark-brown hair, and he released a heavy breath. "I wish there were another way," he breathed out, his voice laced with the bitter tang of regret. He paced toward the balcony, and his gaze became lost in the sprawling landscape.

"This heart condition has taken so much from me in such a short space of time," he sighed as his hand came up to rub the spot just over his heart.

Trish rose from the chair this time and walked over to join him. "I know it's not the most ideal situation, but think about all you still have," she spoke softly.

Paul remained silent for a while; the only sound filling the silence was the harmonious chirping of the distant birds. "I am thankful for all that I do have, especially Sarah."

Trish's lips turned up in a smile at the mention of his daughter. "She is a remarkable young woman and very lucky to have you." The smile faded as rapidly as it had surfaced, replaced by a far-off look. Her lips faded into a gentle frown; her blue eyes became pools of longing. She felt Paul's gaze piercing into the side of her face.

"How is the search going?" His question hung in the air, heavy and full of concern.

"Honestly?" Her eyes met his briefly before returning to the comfort of the picturesque horizon. "I'm conflicted..." Releasing a long breath, she straightened up and gripped the banister for support. "On one hand, I'm hoping Greg has good news, but on the other hand, I don't know if I'm doing the right thing trying to know," she explained.

Paul turned fully to her, compelling her to turn to him. His eyes shone with understanding.

"I can't pretend to know the turmoil you're going through, but I do believe you're making the right choice wanting to know," he encouraged.

Trish's lips turned up in gratitude. "Thanks. I really needed to hear that."

"Anytime, kiddo," Paul responded with a friendly pat on her shoulder.

The insistent hum of her phone against the petite wicker table drew her attention. "Excuse me." She walked over and swiped the device from the table before bringing it closer to read the Caller ID. Her heart pounded like a wild drum in her chest at the name displayed. It was Greg, her private investigator. If he was calling, it meant he had news. As she pressed the answer button, her hand trembled, an echo of her racing heart.

"Hello?" Trish's voice trembled with uncertainty, her fingers tightly gripping the phone.

"Hi, Trish. I hope I haven't caught you at a bad time," the voice at the other end greeted.

"No, not at all," she stammered. Noticing Paul's curious gaze, she silently mouthed the word *"Greg."*

Paul nodded and came closer.

"I found her."

Greg's words hung in the air, carrying a weight that Trish could almost feel physically. A mixture of relief and anxiety washed over her like the ocean tide at the news.

"Hello? Trish? Are you still there?" Greg's voice echoed in her ear; his tone filled with a sense of urgency.

She drew in a deep breath, her mind racing to catch up with the conversation. "I'm sorry. What were you saying?" she finally managed to breathe out.

"I was wondering if you had time to meet with me later. I would rather go through the full disclosure with you in person," the PI expressed, his words measured and composed.

That was just over two hours away.

"Yes. I am," she readily supplied, despite the nervous flutter in her chest.

"All right then. I will be at my office by seven. You can come any time after that."

"Okay. I'll be there."

Trish turned wide-eyed to Paul, whose expectant gaze mirrored her own anticipation.

"Greg said he found her."

"That's, that's...wow!" Paul exclaimed; his voice tinged with genuine excitement. "So what do you do now?"

"I'm meeting him later to get all the details."

"Trish. This is amazing. I'm so happy for you." Paul's smile broadened, warmth radiating from his expression.

Trish returned his smile, happy the day had finally come, but the niggling doubt still remained.

After Paul left, Trish made her way over to the Nestled Inn with the intention of throwing herself into work, in order to keep her mind off her upcoming meeting.

As she approached, her eyes were drawn to the grandeur that stood before her. The three-story structure loomed, a majestic fusion of wood and stone, seemingly defying gravity with its unwavering presence. Gabled roofs soared toward the heavens, while the second floor consisted of a series of elegant balconies boasting secrets of whispered conversations and stolen glances. Large French windows, like portals to another world, beckoned with their translucent charm. The wide, ornate doors were carefully made and added a touch of elegance to the whole picture.

She walked up the few steps that led to the front door and was immediately met by the manager and receptionist for the inn.

"Hi, Trish. Are you here for the grocery list? To be honest, I haven't made it yet, and Dorothy needs to give me a list of the cleaning supplies we are running low on, but I'll get right on that," the small, rosy-cheeked woman spoke a mile a minute, not giving Trish the opportunity to respond.

"Kaylyn," Trish chuckled as she held up her hand to halt the flurry of activities from her. "It's fine. There's no need to rush. I'm not here for the list," she reassured. "I'm here for you to put me to work."

"Oh," Kaylyn replied, her brows furrowed, trying to

figure out what she meant. "What did you have in mind?" she asked cautiously.

"Is there any room that needs to be prepared for the next guest? Is there laundry to be done? I just need something to occupy my time and my mind."

"Well, the Tremaines, who were in the standard double room, checked out this morning, and it needs to be prepared for the guests arriving at five."

"Great. I'll get right on it," Trish said, already heading toward the supply closet. The woman stared in confusion at her retreating back.

Trish spent the next hour scrubbing the bathroom, changing out the mats, and replacing the used towels with clean ones, along with a replenished sample-sized shower gel and shampoo. She then moved on to the bedroom, stripping the four-poster bed and spraying it with Lysol before spreading a clean set of sheets and comforter over it. For the most part, it kept her mind preoccupied from thinking about what was to come in a few hours.

"Trish. Is everything okay?"

Trish glanced over her shoulder to see Kaylyn standing by the door to the laundry room, staring back at her with concern.

"Yeah, why do you ask?" She turned to look at the woman.

"Well, for one, you've been standing over the washing machine for the past five minutes, not moving an inch, and you've been cleaning nonstop since you got here. You only get like this when something's bothering you," Kaylyn responded.

Lines pulled at the corners of Trish's mouth. "You know me so well," she surmised.

Kaylyn gave a sharp nod as her arms came up to fold over her chest. "Now, what's wrong?"

Trish released a sharp breath. "I'm meeting with the private investigator at seven."

"Does that mean he's found her?" Kaylyn asked, her voice laced with hope.

Trish's head bobbed.

"But that's great, Trish. Why aren't you over the moon about this?" Kaylyn asked with a raised brow.

"I am," Trish rushed to affirm. "It's just that everything's about to change, and I am a little apprehensive about it."

Kaylyn walked up to her and placed a comforting hand on her shoulder. "Everything is about to change, but I believe it's all going to work out." Trish gave her friend a grateful smile.

By the time she was finished helping out at the Nestled Inn, it was time to head out to her meeting with Greg. The closer she got to his office, the more anxious she felt.

For years, Trish had been haunted by the decision she made twenty-one years ago, and this news brought her one step closer to the closure she desperately needed. Her mind drifted back to that fateful day at her parents' house.

"How could you be so stupid?"

Trish cringed, her chin tucked into her chest as shame and trepidation filled her.

"All my life, I tried to steer you on the right path to make sure you made something of your life, and this is the thanks I get?"

She peeked from under her lashes, watching her father pace back and forth in anger. Her mother sat on the sofa, a look of helplessness on her face.

Her father stopped pacing and turned to her, his face a sea of rage as he pierced her with riotous blue eyes. "Did you even stop to think what this scandal would do to my reputation?" he seethed. "Answer me!"

She cowered at his booming voice. "I-I'm sorry, Daddy," she whispered as tears splashed her cheeks.

"You're not sorry yet. There is no way you're carrying that—" he pointed at her stomach with a look of disgust— "abomination into this world. You're getting an abortion."

"No!" "Stew!" Trish and her mother exclaimed at the same time.

After all this time, the memory still brought tears to her eyes as she remembered how the freedom of choice was taken away from her. Now, with the possibility of finally meeting her daughter within reach, Trish felt a renewed sense of hope. She wiped the tears from her eyes and took a deep breath, preparing for the emotional journey that lay ahead.

The sun was beginning to set as Trish descended Camano Hill Road. The quiet countryside was bathed in the warm glow of the evening light. But as she rounded a bend, a sudden flash of headlights caught her eye.

A Ford pickup truck, driven by a man whose blood-shot eyes and slurred speech would later reveal him to be heavily intoxicated, barreled toward her at high speed. There was no time to react, no time to swerve out of the way.

The deafening sound of metal on metal echoed through the air as the truck slammed into her car. The force of the impact sent her vehicle flipping through the air, a horrifying ballet of twisted metal and shattered glass. It finally came to a crashing halt against a stone wall, the car now barely recognizable as the mangled wreckage smoked and groaned.

Bleeding and barely conscious, Trish's thoughts turned to the daughter she would never get to meet. Tears streamed down her face, mingling with the blood and dirt that covered her bruised skin. As the darkness closed in around her, she whispered a silent prayer, hoping that somewhere out there, her daughter would know how much she loved her.

And then, everything went black.

Chapter One

Trish's heart raced as she gripped the steering wheel tightly, her knuckles turning white. The night seemed to darken around her, amplifying the fear that gripped her like icy tendrils as the desolate road stretched out before her.

Suddenly, a deafening roar shattered the tranquility of the night. The sound of an engine revving at full throttle pierced through her eardrums, growing louder with every second. Her eyes widened in terror as she stared ahead. A monstrous blue Ford pickup came hurtling toward her, its headlights blazing like twin fiery orbs.

Time seemed to slow down, elongating each agonizing second. Her heart pounded with a desperate rhythm, drowning out the cacophony of her racing thoughts. Sweat soaked her brow as her mind struggled to process the imminent danger that loomed closer, threatening to consume her.

The truck grew larger and more menacing, its metallic frame glistening under the pale moonlight. The revving engine reverberated through the air, a haunting symphony of impending doom. The truck's grating roar drowned out all other sounds, its thunderous crescendo seeping deep into Trish's bones, filling her with overwhelming dread.

Through the windshield of her car, Trish caught a glimpse of the driver's face. Bloodshot eyes, wide and manic, stared back at her, reflecting a feral hunger for chaos. His face was contorted, a sadistic grin etched upon lips that seemed twisted by malevolence.

Desperation clawed at Trish's throat, stifling her scream before it could escape. Her breath came in shallow gasps, her vision narrowing into a tunnel as adrenaline surged through her veins. Time, once crawling, now accelerated with a vengeance, propelling her into a waking nightmare from which there was no escape.

In a sudden explosion of sound and fury, the truck thundered toward her, closing the distance with terrifying speed. The world around her blurred into a chaotic frenzy of lights and colors, a twisted canvas of impending destruction. Her heart pounded against her rib cage, a primal drumbeat of terror.

Then, with a bone-shattering impact, the truck careened into her car, metal colliding with metal in a symphony of destruction. Glass shattered, fragments scattering through the air like malevolent confetti. The violent force propelled Trish forward, her body lurching against the tight embrace of her seat belt, pain shooting through her every nerve ending.

As the deafening collision unleashed its fury, Trish was jolted awake with a start.

Gasping for breath, she realized it had all been a terrifying dream, her racing thoughts merging with the reality of her bedroom. Slowly, she glanced around, seeking solace in the familiar sights and sounds that anchored her to the safety of the waking world. Yet, even as she calmed her racing heart, the memory of the blue Ford and the driver behind the wheel still lingered and caused an involuntary shudder to run through her body.

Beads of sweat trickled down her temples as her heart pounded against her chest. It was the same nightmare that haunted her night after night, an exaggerated version of the accident that had changed her life forever.

Four months had passed since that fateful day, but the memories were as fresh as ever. Trish had woken up from her coma two months later, her body broken and her spirit shattered. The physical wounds were healing, thanks to the relentless effort of physical therapy, but the emotional scars ran deep.

As Trish took deep breaths, trying to steady her racing heartbeat, her eyes tried to adjust to the room bathed in darkness, save for the faint glow of the moon peering through the curtains. She gingerly touched the scar on her forehead, tracing the uneven texture with her fingertips. It was a constant reminder of what she had gone through, a visible symbol of the pain she carried within.

She dragged herself out of bed, her movements slightly hindered by the lingering effects of the accident. She walked with a slight limp, her body still adjusting to the trauma it had endured. But she was determined not to let her physical limitations slow her down.

In front of the mirror, she studied her reflection. Disappointment weighed down her lips.

There was a gentle knock on her door, followed by the sound of it creaking open. Nikki's concerned face peeked through the gap. "Hey," she said softly. "I was just heading to the kitchen to get a glass of water, and I noticed your light was on. Are you okay?"

Trish's lips pinched upward, a forced attempt at a smile. "Mhm hmm," she responded tightly, hoping to dismiss her sister's worry.

Nikki's eyes narrowed slightly as if trying to see through the facade Trish was trying to maintain. Stepping fully into the room, she closed the door behind her. "Uh oh. That doesn't sound like you're fine," she said, her voice filled with genuine concern. "What's wrong?"

Trish's frustration bubbled to the surface, mingling with her pain. She turned to face her sister. "Nikki, I'm fine," she reiterated, her voice rising.

Nikki took a step closer, her voice gentle and soothing. "Trish, I'm only trying to help."

A surge of anger shot through Trish's veins, fueling her words. "Well, I didn't ask for your help," she snapped, her voice laced with bitterness. Her gaze met Nikki's through the mirror, their eyes locking in a battle of emotions. "Why can't you just leave me be for once? Can't you understand I just need to be alone right now?"

Noticing her sister's wide-eyed stare and the way her lips trembled, Trish's anger began to dissipate, leaving behind a tinge of regret. She drew in a tight breath, her eyes fluttering shut as she struggled to rein in her emotions. "I'm sorry. I didn't mean to snap at you," she finally admitted, her voice now tinged with vulnerability. "I just..."

Nikki's voice, gentle and filled with understanding, interrupted her, "Did you have another nightmare?"

Trish's eyes widened at the question. Nikki watched her with seriousness in her eyes. She sighed, her shoulders slumping. Turning away from the mirror, her gaze fixed on a spot on the bed. "It felt so real, Nikki," she confirmed in a shaky voice. "It always does. I could hear the screeching tires, the crashing metal, my body slamming against the door... I woke up feeling like it just happened all over again." She released a dejected sigh.

Nikki took a tentative step forward, reaching out a hand as if to offer comfort. "Trish, you don't have to face this alone. I know it's hard, but shutting everyone out won't make the nightmares go away. I'm here for you, Amy's here for you—no matter what."

She hesitated, her gaze flickering between Nikki's outstretched hand and her own trembling fingers. Slowly, she reached out, allowing their hands to intertwine.

"I... I know it's not fair to push you away. God knows I've done that often enough," she admitted, her voice laced with a newfound vulnerability. "I just need time to sort out all the noise in my head."

Nikki nodded in understanding. "I get that. I do...I just want you to remember—you're not alone—not anymore."

Trish's lips lifted in a smile, and Nikki returned it before heading for the door. Trish turned her attention back to the mirror and grimaced before sighing.

"You're beautiful, Trish."

Her lips parted, startled by her sister's voice. She hadn't realized she was still there. Nikki's blue eyes looked over Trish's shoulder at her reflection in the mirror.

Trish turned to face her sister, her eyes brimming with tears. "We must be seeing two different things then because every time I look in the mirror, all I see is this hideous scar on my face. I'm just a broken woman, marked by scars and haunted by nightmares," she choked up.

Nikki's expression softened, and she enveloped Trish

in a warm embrace. "Trish, that's not true. You are beautiful." Trish shook her head vigorously against her sister's chest. "It is true. You are beautiful," Nikki reiterated. "I know it's hard for you to believe right now, but your beauty shines from within. The strength you've shown in overcoming this tragedy, the way you've fought to regain your life—that's what makes you truly beautiful."

Trish clung to her sister, her tears mingling with Nikki's comforting touch. At that moment, she allowed herself to believe that maybe, just maybe, she could find beauty in her imperfections.

The knock on the door interrupted their embrace, causing them to turn their attention there. It creaked open, revealing a young woman standing hesitantly in the doorway. Her sandy-blond hair with ombre highlights was the same shade as Trish's, as were her light blue eyes set in an oval face, and her straight nose and slightly fuller lips were an exact replica. Her brows furrowed with concern, and her eyes scanned the room before settling on the two women.

"Is everything okay?" Her tentative steps barely made a sound as she hovered, her body leaning slightly forward. Her fingers gently grazed the doorknob, a subtle display of her unease, as she awaited a response.

"Yeah, sweetie. I was just checking to see if your mom needed anything. I'm headed to get a drink from the kitchen," Nikki answered before Trish could respond. "You couldn't sleep either?"

"Um... no. I needed a drink of water myself." Her eyes flickered to her mother. "I could get you a drink if you want," she offered.

"Thank you, Amy, but I'm fine," Trish responded with a grateful smile.

Her daughter's lips turned up slightly before turning to her aunt. "You want me to get that water to you?"

"Uh...no. That's fine," Nikki reassured her. "I have a better idea. Why don't we all go to the kitchen and maybe have some hot chocolate or fudge?" Her eyes lit up with expectation.

"I don't know," Trish hesitated. "I'm still very tired, and it's only 3 a.m."

"It's okay. I'm tired too. I just needed the water, then I'm heading back to bed," Amy jumped up. "I'll see you both in the morning." With that, she hurried toward the door.

Trish watched helplessly as her daughter slipped through the door. She longed to make up for the lost years, to forge a bond with Amy that could withstand the weight of their shared history.

It wasn't an easy task. Amy was guarded, her heart shielded by months of uncertainty and unanswered questions, and Trish was afraid of doing or saying the wrong thing. Yet it seemed like that's all she had been doing for the past two months since she met her.

"What was that?" Nikki held her hands before her as she stared incredulously at Trish.

Chapter Two

Trish wrapped the shawl tightly around her shoulders as she settled into her favorite wicker seat on the porch, enjoying the scene before her as the rays of the evening sun showed through the foliage of evergreens standing tall on the outskirts of the property. The wind whistled and carried a hint of autumn's arrival. Pretty soon, the leaves would be an array of oranges, reds, and yellows, and the air a crisp, cool bite.

She closed her eyes for a moment, allowing her senses to fully absorb the ambiance surrounding her. The sound of the front door opening caused her to turn her head in its direction.

"I brought you some hot cider," Amy announced, stepping through the door with a warm smile on her lips.

"Thanks, sweetie," Trish replied, her cheeks warming from her smile. She extended her hand to take the mug. Steam rose from the rim, and the spicy aroma of the cider mingling with the earthy scent of the season infiltrated her nostrils as she brought it close.

Her daughter settled into an empty chair beside her.

Trish brought the mug to her lips and took a sip of the tangy beverage infused with cinnamon, cloves, and a hint of something she couldn't quite put her finger on. A contented sigh left her lips.

"Good, right?" Amy asked with a knowing grin, her eyes twinkling.

"It is," Trish smiled, then took another sip. "So good," she reiterated. "I'm tasting the cinnamon and cloves, but there's something else."

Amy leaned forward in her direction, causing Trish to lean toward her. "It's a secret." She smirked.

"Ah, you tricked me," Trish chuckled. Her daughter joined in, the sound of her laughter warming Trish's heart. She liked moments like these with Amy.

They sat in comfortable silence, sipping their cider. Breaking the silence, Trish asked, "How's culinary school going?"

Amy's face lit up, her eyes shining with infectious enthusiasm. "It's great. I'm learning so much." Her voice danced with an undercurrent of enthusiasm. "It's like stepping into a magical realm of flavors and techniques."

Trish couldn't help but be drawn into Amy's contagious passion. She leaned closer, her ears attuned to the words falling from her daughter's mouth and a soft smile curving her lips.

"I'm learning the art of delicate gelling technique. My professor says I'm pretty close to mastering it, and he's never had a student catch on so fast."

"Really? Wow. That's incredible," Trish complimented, a proud smile on her face. Amy beamed.

"I remember when I was younger, about twelve, living with my parents..." She faltered, uncertainty swimming in her eyes, "...adopted parents, I would try and recreate dishes from the cooking channel." She chuckled as her eyes glazed over in memory. "Mom would always encourage me and say it was good, even when it wasn't. She always used to tell me I was going to be one heck of a chef."

Trish's heart clenched at the mention of another woman being called "mom," but she pushed the feeling away. "It is a fact, you are going to be a great pastry chef. I can't wait for you to open your own patisserie and get those Michelin stars."

Amy smiled appreciatively.

"What about your adopted father? " she ventured.

"What about him?"

"Well. I've heard you talk about your mother but not him. I was just curious about what he thought of you wanting to become a chef," Trish explained.

Amy's expression changed, then a shadow crossed her features. "He wasn't around much," she said in a clipped tone.

The change wasn't lost on Trish. She felt a pang of guilt, a reminder of the years she hadn't been there for Amy. "And how was he when he was around?" she questioned, her heart pounding.

"He didn't believe in my dream, I guess," Amy replied with a shrug of her shoulder.

"How so?" Trish pushed. She already had an idea about the type of man her father had been from the PI's report and what Nikki had told her, but for some reason, she wanted Amy to tell her. She wanted her to feel comfortable sharing these things with her.

Amy's eyes hardened. "I don't want to talk about it, okay? Not everyone gets to choose where they end up when they're not wanted."

The words hit Trish like a physical blow. "I'm...I'm sorry, Amy," she said, her voice choked with emotion. "I shouldn't have pushed."

Amy released a heavy breath and looked straight ahead as she spoke, "I'm sorry. Talking about my dad, it's a really sore spot for me."

"You don't have to apologize. I understand," Trish assured her. "I'm the one who made the choice all those years ago to give you up for adoption."

Amy glanced at her before facing forward once more.

Trish drew air into her lungs before releasing it and continuing, "In my mind at the time, you would've been adopted by a family that loved you very much and gave you everything I couldn't. I..." Trish's shoulders deflated as the air whooshed through her lips. "I didn't think for a minute it would have ever been anything different."

"Yeah. Well, there's no point crying over spilled milk now. Is there? I didn't get a fairy-tale story. Instead, I ended up with a father who was an abusive drunk and a mother too scared to do anything about it." Amy's voice was thick with emotion.

"Amy..." Trish reached over and placed a comforting hand on the girl's shoulder, her own heart breaking at the thought that her daughter had been hurt by the people who should have been protecting her. She wanted to pull her into her arms, but she was afraid it would only cause her daughter to push her away. She watched as Amy's throat worked with emotion, and a tear slipped down her cheek.

"I'm gonna go inside." Amy stood abruptly, her chair scraping harshly against the wooden porch. She reached down and took the now empty mugs in her hand, and turned toward the door.

Trish watched helplessly as Amy walked across the porch to the door and disappeared inside. She remained seated, staring unseeingly out at the lawn. Her mind was a whirl of thoughts and feelings. Her relationship with Amy was fragile, like a thin sheet of ice over a deep, dark lake. Try hard as she may to get closer to her; it only seemed her steps were causing cracks in the ice that could shatter at any moment and plunge them both into the frigid depths of uncertainty. She didn't realize she was crying until she felt the droplet against the back of her hand.

Feeling the need to try and comfort her daughter, Trish got up and slowly made her way inside to find Amy. She froze at the sight of Amy wrapped in Nikki's warm embrace. A bitter pang of jealousy twisted inside her. She felt like an outsider in her own home, watching a moment she longed to be a part of but had no right to.

She retreated to the porch, sinking into her chair, her gaze tracing the verdant landscape awash with the glow of the evening sun, a contrast to the bleakness she felt inside. She had found her daughter after twenty-one years, but she was still a stranger—the one looking in.

The evening air was growing colder, but Trish didn't mind. She sat on the porch, alone with her thoughts, pondering the fragility of the relationship she was trying to rebuild.

The sound of tires crunching on the gravel caught her attention, and her gaze cut to the driveway, just as a black SUV came to a stop before the house. Her heart lurched with a mixture of anticipation and nervousness as Reed emerged from the driver's side. Slowly, she eased her way out of her chair and walked over to stand by the steps, leaning against the porch column for support and to steady her racing pulse.

A tender smile curved Reed's lips as his gray eyes locked on to her. Her heart fluttered even faster within her chest. With a couple of purposeful strides, he ascended the porch steps, closing the distance between them.

"Hi, Trish," Reed greeted, his voice carrying a hint of warmth and familiarity.

"Reed...this is a surprise. I wasn't expecting you," she replied, a smile illuminating her features as she looked up at him.

"I know. I just thought I would check up on you and see how you were doing. This isn't a bad time, is it?" Reed's voice carried a touch of concern as he approached her. His hands slid effortlessly into the front pockets of his jeans, a subtle gesture that exuded both casualness and eagerness. He shifted his weight from one foot to another, his body language mirroring his anticipation as he awaited her response.

Her eyes flickered with surprise and a hint of delight. "Um, no. It's not. I was just sitting out here, relishing the change in weather," she expressed, a soft smile playing at the corners of her lips. "My leg was starting to feel a bit stiff though, so I suppose it's a good thing you showed up; otherwise, I wouldn't be able to move." She chuckled, the sound carrying a note of self-amusement.

Reed's chuckle resonated warmly, reverberating in his chest. His eyes crinkled at the edges, mirroring the genuine joy that danced within him. But after a couple of seconds, his expression turned more serious; his gaze fixated on her injured leg. "Glad I could help," he said, his voice maintaining a lightness yet tinged with a deeper concern.

He took a step closer, his eyes lingering on her with a mixture of tenderness and curiosity. "How is the leg?" he asked with genuine concern.

She shifted her weight, her healing leg moving back and forth, a gentle rhythm of progress. Her eyes met his, a flicker of gratitude shimmering within their depths. "It's not so bad," she replied, her voice laced with a quiet resilience. "As long as I diligently do the stretches I learned in physical therapy and avoid staying in a sitting position for too long, I manage," she explained. Her fingers absently traced invisible patterns on her thigh.

"That's good. I'm happy it's healing well." Reed smiled tenderly at her.

Trish felt goosebumps prickle her skin and a stirring in her chest. She ducked her head. She could feel his gaze still on her, and she felt heat rising up her neck. Pretty soon, her cheeks would be a bright red.

"Why don't we sit on the porch swing? It's higher than the other chairs, so maybe it could take some of the pressure off your leg," he suggested.

"Yeah. Okay," she responded, her voice a little breathless.

They slowly made their way toward the porch swing, Reed patiently following behind her as she navigated with her healing leg, causing her to walk slower than usual. The feel of his hand at the small of her back and on her forearm as he helped her settle on the swing caused goosebumps on her skin once more and her cheeks to burn red. He settled beside her; their bodies close yet comfortably distant. The creaking of the swing echoed in the silence, harmonizing with the rhythm of Trish's heart.

She stole a sideways glance at him. His face was bathed in the soft glow of the setting sun. Her heart fluttered as she observed the play of light and shadow on his strong jawline as the warm hues highlighted the contours of his face.

He turned quickly, his gray eyes trapping her in their alluring glow. His lips curled into a gentle smile that sent a ripple of warmth through her.

Trish's heart raced, her mind swirling with a thousand questions. She had always sensed the undercurrent of their attraction to each other, but neither of them had been brave enough to act on it. However, ever since her accident, Reed had become extra attentive, and she could sense he was getting ready to tell her how he felt about her.

At that moment, the porch swing became more than just a seat; it became a sanctuary where their souls danced in harmony and where the boundaries between friendship and something deeper blurred into the realm of possibility.

"How is Amy?"

Just like that, the serenity was shattered, replaced by the despair from earlier.

Chapter Three

Amy tightened the laces of her hiking boots and secured the small fanny pack at her waist as she set foot on the Marine Loop Trail. The cool air nipped at her cheeks, urging her to pull her jacket tighter around her. She took a deep breath, filling her lungs with the scent of damp earth and fallen leaves, and began her solitary trek.

As she walked along the trail, the sound of her footsteps on the crunchy foliage provided a steady rhythm. The dense forest enveloped her in a comforting embrace, its towering evergreens creating a canopy overhead. Sunlight filtered through the branches, casting dappled shadows on the moss-covered ground.

She paused for a moment, leaning against a gnarled tree trunk. Closing her eyes, she allowed the gentle rustling of leaves and the distant chirping of birds to serenade her. In this tranquil moment, she found solace and sought answers to the questions that lingered in her mind.

Lost in her thoughts, she was startled by the sound of approaching footsteps. She turned and saw an elderly couple. They smiled warmly at her, their eyes twinkling with the joy of the outdoors.

"Beautiful day for a hike, isn't it?" the man said, his voice carrying the melody of contentment.

Amy returned the smile. "Yes, it truly is. This place is breathtaking."

The woman nodded, her gaze sweeping across the forest floor. "Autumn always paints nature in its most splendid palette. It's a reminder that change can be beautiful."

Amy's eyes followed the couple as they continued their leisurely stroll along the trail. She was grateful for the short intrusion of their words. As she ventured deeper into the trail, the temperature dropped further, causing her breath to form a faint mist in the air. She zipped up her jacket and quickened her pace to generate some warmth. The path wound its way through a grove of maple trees, their leaves fluttering like delicate confetti in the breeze.

In the distance, the tranquil lapping of waves reached her ears, a testament to the trail's proximity to the ocean. Amy veered off the main path and followed a narrow trail that led down to the shoreline. The salty scent of the sea mingled with the earthy fragrance of the forest. It was the most natural scent she had ever experienced.

She found a spot on a weathered driftwood log, the perfect perch to look out at the vastness of the ocean before her. Seagulls soared overhead, their cries breaking the silence of the beach.

The rhythmic crashing of the waves against the shore provided a comforting backdrop to the turmoil within her mind. Trish's question about her adoptive father had stirred up emotions she had desperately tried to bury—memories that left her scarred.

She clenched her fists, feeling the anger and hurt welling up inside her. How could she let him still have such control over her? The memories flooded back, unbidden and unwelcomed. She remembered the venomous words he had hurled at her in his drunken rage—the way they had cut through her like shards of glass.

"You'll never amount to anything... You're nothing without your mother and me... I wish you were never born..." The words transformed in meaning after discovering she had been adopted.

Amy closed her eyes, and suddenly, the scene played out vividly in her mind like a haunting flashback. The memory transported her back to that fateful night, the night she had summoned every ounce of courage within her to call the police on him. She found herself standing in the dimly lit living room, her heart pounding in her chest.

Her hands clenched into tight fists, her face a mask of determination.

She stepped forward, her voice steady, despite the fear that threatened to consume her. "That's enough! Leave her alone!"

He turned toward Amy, his bloodshot eyes filled with rage and a hint of surprise. "You little brat! Mind your own business!" he spat, his words slurring together.

"I won't let you hurt her anymore," Amy said, her voice quivering with a combination of fear and defiance. She reached for her phone, her fingers trembling as she dialed the emergency number.

As the call connected, Amy's breath caught in her

throat. *The operator's voice filled the room, calm and reas-suring. "911, what's your emergency?"*

Tears streamed down Amy's face as she struggled to speak. "P-please, you have to come quickly. My mom... he's hurting her."

The arrival of the police had been a blur of flashing lights and chaotic voices. She watched as they wrestled her father to the ground, handcuffing him with a firmness that matched the weight of his actions. The sound of the car door slamming shut echoed in her ears, as they shuttled him away from their shattered home and into the cold confines of the police vehicle.

The neighbors had been drawn to the commotion like moths to a flame. Amy could remember their curious faces, peering out from porches and curtains, their eyes filled with a mix of concern and satisfaction. It was as if their private tragedy had become a public spectacle—an event to be witnessed and whispered about.

But what stung the most, what brought the tears streaming down her face, was the look she had seen in her mother's eyes that night. It wasn't gratitude or relief. Instead, it was a potent blend of anger and disappointment directed squarely at her. Amy had called the police to protect her mother, to shield her from harm, but the gesture had been met with a silent accusation.

Amy's tears mingled with the briny ocean air as she continued to stare out, her vision blurred. The crashing waves seemed to echo the turmoil in her heart—a constant reminder of the pain she had endured and the scars that still lingered.

Minutes turned into hours as Amy lost track of time, lost in the pain and anguish that came with growing up the way she did. Her innocence had been marred by one disappointment after the other—now she was waiting for it to extend to her newly minted relationship with Trish and Nikki.

She retraced her steps along the Marine Loop Trail and got in her car to head home.

* * *

"Your cabernet sauvignon, Mr. Graham." Amy presented the bottle of expensive red wine before expertly pouring the ruby liquid into a crystal glass.

"Thank you, Amy," the man replied with a warm smile. She smiled and took a step back as she waited for him to take a sip of his drink. "Excellent." He nodded in approval, setting the glass flat on the table. Amy moved forward then and halved the glass of wine before setting the bottle down.

"Your meal will be out shortly," she informed him before stepping away from the table and making her way back to the kitchen.

Back in the kitchen, the climate was a stark contrast to the refined dining room of Lot 28. It was a symphony of chaos and artistry as the skilled chefs worked hard to create the masterpieces that ensured they maintained their Michelin status, all under the watchful eye of the head chef, Doug.

Waitressing was second nature to her. She had been doing it for nearly four years now, and Lot 28 had become her refuge. The bustling, the noise, and the rhythm kept out her intrusive thoughts. But as the day aged, the mask began to crack. Her thoughts, intrusive and unbidden, gnawed at her.

"Order up, Amy!" Doug barked, his voice cutting through the clatter of pots and pans.

Amy jolted back to reality. "Yes, Chef." Lifting the tray, she headed for the dining hall once more.

"I didn't order this." The woman looked up with a brow arched in question.

"I am so sorry. I'll have it replaced," Amy apologized, lifting the dish from the table. Pushing the double doors, she entered the kitchen. "Doug," she stammered, her voice trembling, "I...I messed up the order for table seven."

Doug paused, his stern face softening as he looked at her. "Everything okay, Amy?" he asked, his gruff voice unusually gentle.

"Yes, Doug. I'm okay." Amy responded, a tentative smile on her lips. "I...I won't mess up again," she assured him, but her voice lacked conviction.

Doug looked at her for a long time. Amy held her breath. "All right, but be careful next time," he warned.

After correcting the order at table seven, Amy continued working. As she made her way toward the kitchen once more, she tripped. Before the tray could clatter to the floor, a hand shot out to catch it and steady her. "Whoa there," Paul cautioned.

"You okay?" His words, though well-intentioned, felt like salt on her raw emotions.

She responded mechanically, "Yes," barely meeting his concerned gaze.

"Take a break, kiddo," he suggested, his tone softer now.

But his words provoked her, and she retorted harshly, "I'm fine. I can do my job."

"I didn't say you couldn't." Paul raised his hands.

31

"I don't need you treating me special just because you and Nikki are dating," she huffed out. "I'm not some charity case."

"Amy," Paul said in a calming tone as he rested his hand comfortingly on her shoulder. "If it was any of my other staff, I would have given them the same instruction because I care about their well-being," he reasoned. "And I care about you. It's okay to let people care about you."

Amy's lips lifted in an apologetic smile. "I'm sorry for snapping at you."

"It's okay," Paul smiled. Tilting his head so their eyes met, he instructed, "Take a break. I insist."

"Okay. Thanks, Paul." Amy pushed open the back door, stepping out into the warm afternoon sunlight. The noise of clinking glasses and murmuring customers faded behind her. As she made her way toward a secluded corner of the restaurant's patio, she noticed a young woman approaching.

"Sarah," Amy smiled widely.

Sarah smiled warmly at her. "I saw you talking to Dad before you came out and thought I'd check if you were okay. You looked really upset. What happened?"

Amy sighed; her frustration evident. "It's nothing, really...just a niggling feeling this new life I have won't last, and I am constantly waiting for the other shoe to drop."

Sarah nodded empathetically, her expression mirroring Amy's concern. She reached out and gently squeezed Amy's hand, offering comfort. "You deserve happiness, Amy. Sometimes, our minds trick us into doubting the good things that come our way. It's natural to be cautious, but don't let fear overshadow the joy in your life," she encouraged.

Amy's brow furrowed as she looked down at her trembling hands. "I know, but sometimes I wish I hadn't found out I was adopted. I wish I hadn't met Trish and Nikki and all these nice people. It feels like it can all disappear just as quickly, and I'm used to disappointment."

Sarah stepped closer, placing a comforting hand on Amy's arm. "Amy, those people love you—a lot. They're not letting you go. I love you too. In the short time I've known you, you have proven to be a wonderful, caring person and friend.

Amy looked up at Sarah, tears shimmering in her eyes. She searched Sarah's face for any sign of insincerity but found only warmth and understanding. Slowly, a small smile tugged at the corners of her lips. "Thanks, Sarah. I appreciate your friendship too. So, how's the little one doing?" she asked, her eyes sparkling with anticipation as she changed the subject.

Sarah's hand instinctively rested on her barely noticeable baby bump, even at three months. "My little Buttercup is doing great," she replied, her voice filled with a mixture of awe and tenderness. "In fact, Aaron and I had an ultrasound just yesterday. We got to see our little bundle of joy squirming around. It was such an incredible experience."

Amy's eyes widened with delight. "That's amazing!" she exclaimed. "I can only imagine how awesome it must have been to see your baby moving. It's like a glimpse into the future, isn't it?"

A soft smile graced Sarah's lips. "It truly was," she agreed. "Seeing that tiny, growing life inside me made everything feel so real."

"Growing a life is such a wonderful gift," Amy smiled. A wave of melancholy passed over her. She felt

Sarah's hand on her arm apply pressure, and she smiled gratefully.

"Everything will work out okay for you, Amy," Sarah encouraged.

Amy gave her a grateful smile. She hoped her friend was right.

Chapter Four

"Miss Parker, you are late. This is the third time in two weeks." Chef Reynolds peered at Amy over his thin, wire-rimmed glasses from the front of the class.

"I'm sorry, Chef," Amy apologized, suspended by the door.

Her words were rushed and breathless. She hurriedly pushed her hands through the sleeves of her chef coat and quickly buttoned it.

Chef Reynolds's eyes never left her, piercing through like a precision-carved knife. Folding his arms over the well-tailored chef's coat he wore, he spoke. "Need I remind you of the expectations of this kitchen?" His voice carried an undercurrent of disappointment.

Amy's heart sank, and she lowered her gaze, unable to meet his piercing stare. "No, Chef," she murmured, her voice barely above a whisper. "It won't happen again, I promise."

Chef Reynolds leaned forward, his intense stare narrowing even further. "Regardless, Miss Parker," he began, his voice firm. "I feel the need to remind you the business of becoming the best at what you do takes long hours of training and attention to detail, which cannot be achieved if you are giving away the time that should be spent learning what it takes to not just be good but to be the best."

Amy's heart sank deeper, the weight of his words pressing upon her. She understood the truth behind his reprimand, the passion and dedication required to rise above mediocrity. She hadn't meant to be late, but she had slept through her alarm, which meant she had to rush to get ready and drive like a mad woman on the road just to make it to her class on time. The only consolation was it was less than twenty minutes away. She needed a new way of waking up on time.

"Yes, Chef." She bowed her head, hoping it would cast her in a light of humbled servitude and hopefully satisfy her professor.

At the tense silence, she chanced a peek only for her eyes to collide with the steely, gray stare from him.

Professor Reynolds released a weighty sigh. He crooked his finger, gesturing for her to walk to him. "You are a very promising student, Amy, but I need you to be consistent. Is that understood?" he asked, his voice less condescending than it had been earlier.

"Yes, Chef. I understand." She nodded lowly.

"Get to your position. I need to begin the lesson," he instructed before turning to the class. "Today, we will be braiding bread rolls," he announced.

Amy's eyes quickly darted over to the stations to see Jill, one of the few people she had become friends with since starting culinary school a month ago. She quickly walked over to her, and Jill smiled welcomingly before facing the front of the class.

"That was brutal," Jill whispered, offering Amy a sideways glance while their professor explained their baking assignment.

"Tell me about it," Amy whispered discreetly back to her friend.

"I thought he was about to tell you to write a thousand lines on why you should be on time." Jill covered her mouth to try and stifle a snicker, her eyes sparkling with mischief.

"Did I say something funny, Miss Scott?" Their professor's voice sliced through the air; his words laced with a hint of sternness. Jill's brown eyes widened in fear, her posture straightening as she swiftly turned to face him.

"No, Chef," she stammered, her voice tinged with anxiety. "I'm sorry."

"Seems there is a lot of sorry going around," he responded with a disapproving scowl. "I will not be repeating the instructions, so it is in everyone's best interest that you pay attention. Am I understood?"

"Yes, Chef," the class responded in unison.

Amy kept her eyes focused on Professor Reynolds, who had started speaking once more. She could feel the accusatory stares and frowns from her classmates, but she kept her head forward.

"To achieve the utmost softness, you should allow your dough to rest overnight. A good twenty-four hours should be adequate time for it to ferment and develop its flavors." Professor Reynolds expressed that before instructing them to remove the dough he'd had them prepare the day before.

Professor Reynolds proceeded to explain the intricate steps, his words painting vivid images. "To achieve the perfect texture, the conditions under which the bread bakes must be perfect. I know you are all accustomed to baking, but as a chef, the standard of your work has to supersede a mere hobby."

Amy remained attentive, taking in all her professor said, and when it was time to begin, she carefully removed the dough and rolled it out before cutting it into strips and plaiting them the way he had taught them. She then placed the pan in the oven, carefully adjusting the temperature and setting the timer. She stepped back with a satisfied lift of her lips. Minutes ticked by, and anticipation filled the room like a tangible presence.

Finally, the timers started chiming one after the other, signaling the completion of the students' creations. Amy swiftly withdrew the bread, her eyes shining with pride at the texture. She meticulously spread butter across the crust, allowing its warmth to seep into every crevice.

"All right, class. Let's see how well you have done on this assignment," Professor Reynolds spoke before making his rounds to inspect each student's bread.

As Professor Reynolds approached her station, Amy's heart quickened in her chest. His gaze swept over her bread before he took a knife and pocked the top. Amy held her breath.

Slowly, his gaze lifted to Amy. A smile tugged at the corners of his lips, a rare display of satisfaction. "Well done, Amy," he commended, his voice carrying a note of genuine approval.

Amy's lips automatically lifted as her relief and happiness brimmed over. "Thank you, Chef."

With a final nod, Professor Reynolds left Amy to view another student's work.

A hush fell over the room as Chef Reynolds cleared his throat. "I am pleased to say you all did well. I am impressed to see you are paying attention and using all you have been taught."

Murmurs of relief filled the room.

"Now, I have some important news to share with you," he began, his voice carrying a hint of intrigue, "We are in for a delightful treat next week." He paused, creating an air of suspense and piquing the students' interest. "We have managed to secure a guest lecturer, a true prodigy of the pastry world."

Whispers rippled through the room, classmates exchanging nervous glances.

"This rising star," Chef Reynolds continued, "has been hailed as a maestro of confectionery, gracing the pages of the esteemed *Haute Pâtisserie*. Their talent has captivated the taste buds and imagination of gourmands across the western hemisphere."

Amy's mind raced with the possibilities of learning from a world-renowned chef. It would definitely look prestigious on her résumé.

"But," he added, drawing out the word and bringing Amy's attention back to him. "I shall keep their name a secret for now. Let the element of surprise enhance the anticipation."

A chorus of disappointed sighs mingled with the collective curiosity, but Amy couldn't help the thrill that coursed through her. Her fingers tingled with the need to create, to learn from this prodigious talent who would grace their classroom.

"So, who do you think it is?" Jill asked when they exited the kitchen.

"What do you mean?" Amy asked.

"The famous chef, duh," Jill deadpanned.

"I don't know," she shrugged. "There aren't many famous pâtissiers out there, to begin with, but it's still hard to guess something like that," she reasoned.

"I bet it's Wolfgang," Jill said, her voice hopeful.

"He's not a pastry chef, Jill. Why would he come?" Amy chuckled.

"Wishful thinking." Jill grinned.

As the two said their goodbyes, Amy entered her car and drove out of the school's parking lot. Instead of heading home, she made her way onto NE Camano Drive and turned into the parking lot of the Camano Plaza.

As she entered the building, her steps resonated against the polished tiles that adorned the bustling shopping center. The air was laced with a collection of scents, a melange of freshly brewed coffee, fragrant flowers, and the faint hint of warm pastries wafting from a bakery or two. People with shopping bags passed her while others milled about the spacious plaza, contemplating whether they should enter the stores lining the walls. Stepping onto the escalator, she allowed it to transport her to the next floor of the plaza, taking purposeful strides toward the culinary supplies shop and then entered.

The cashier, a young man who looked like he was in his teens, simply looked up from the manga he was reading to glance briefly at her before his head was buried in the book once more.

"Excuse me, could you point me to the baking supplies section?" She walked up to him and asked.

The young man looked up once more, this time

sporting an irritated look. "It's in aisle five, miss," he answered.

"Thank you." Amy gave him a saccharine smile before heading toward the aisle.

As she walked through the aisle, her fingers danced over the array of canvas pastry bags, testing the smooth texture against her skin. Nearby, an assortment of intricate tips beckoned her. She went to take up a set of the icing tips, examining the diameter of the openings.

When she was satisfied with the items she'd chosen, she turned the corner of the aisle, only to bump into something solid that pushed her back. A hand held her by the elbow, keeping her from falling.

"Oh, I'm so sorry," she hurriedly apologized, her voice laced with genuine regret as she regained her balance. Her breath caught in her chest when her eyes lifted to the stranger before her.

He offered a forgiving smile that transformed his face and commanded her attention. She found herself momentarily captivated by his allure. His brown hair brushed his forehead with a carefree elegance, cascading down to the nape of his neck in gentle waves. His piercing green eyes held a glimmer of curiosity, like emerald gems seeking to unravel the mysteries of the world. Towering above her, he exuded an undeniable presence, his height emphasizing his confident demeanor. He was handsome.

"It's all right," he assured her with a warm timbre. His bright smile persisted, infusing the atmosphere with a palpable warmth. "No harm done."

Amy's cheeks flushed with a hint of rosy embarrassment as she found herself caught in the magnetic pull of his gaze. She extended a hand toward him, her heart fluttering like a butterfly preparing for flight.

"I'm Gabriel," the gentleman held out a hand to her in greeting. His eyes sparkled with interest; his curiosity evident in his attentive posture. "I'm new to this island, actually. Just arrived."

"I'm Amy," she introduced herself, her voice a shy whisper as she took the hand he offered. His hand enveloped her smaller one, and warmth traveled up her arm from their contact. She fought an involuntary shiver. Clearing her throat, she spoke up, "I've only been living on Camano Island for a couple of months, but it's truly a slice of heaven. I'm sure you'll like it."

A grin tugged at Gabriel's lips, amplifying his irresistible charm. "I can already see that," he confessed, his words laced with sincere admiration. "And I hope the people here are as nice as you are."

The words hung in the air, momentarily stealing Amy's breath away. A soft blush crept across her cheeks, a testament to Gabriel's effect on her. She found herself momentarily lost in the depths of his gaze.

A customer walking by broke whatever invisible chord had held them captive. "Right. Well, it was great meeting you, Gabriel." Amy smiled.

"Likewise, Amy. I hope this won't be the last time we bump into each other." Gabriel smiled, his eyes shining with intrigue.

Her heart skipped a beat.

Chapter Five

"Miss Parker, Mr. Matthis will see you now."

"Okay. Thank you," Trish responded to the receptionist with a smile, rising to her feet and heading down the corridor. She gingerly stepped into the bright, airy room, the scent of freshly laundered towels mingling with the sterile tang of antiseptic. Sunlight streamed through the large windows, casting warm golden rays across the polished hardwood floor. The walls were adorned with motivational quotes and vibrant posters, encouraging patients to persevere and embrace their journey to recovery.

As she settled onto the padded examination table, her heart swelled with a mixture of anticipation and frustration. Two months had passed since her broken leg had begun to heal, and while progress had been made, her gait still betrayed a lingering limp. The physical therapy sessions had become a bittersweet ritual, a constant reminder of the distance between her current state and the fluid grace of her pre-injury days.

"Good morning, Trish," greeted her physical therapist

with a warm smile. His voice, rich and reassuring, carried a hint of empathy. "How are we feeling today?"

Trish sighed, her voice tinged with a touch of exasperation. "I'm hanging in there, Craig. I'm just frustrated with the pace of my recovery. It's been two months, and I still can't walk without this annoying limp."

Craig nodded, his eyes conveying understanding. "I know it can be discouraging, but healing takes time. Remember, Rome wasn't built in a day. We'll get you back on your feet, I promise. You just have to stick to the routine we've set up. I just need to do a physical check, and then we can head out to the therapy room for your workout." Trish nodded. Fifteen minutes later, they were in a room filled with bars attached to the walls, various types of exercise machines, weights, and dumbbells.

With a gentle yet firm touch, Craig began the session by guiding Trish through a series of exercises. He positioned himself next to her, his reassuring presence giving her a sense of security.

"All right, Trish, let's start with some knee bends," Craig said, adjusting her leg into the proper position. "Bend your knee slowly, feeling the muscles working."

Trish obeyed, her face tensing up as she flexed her knee. The effort caused her thigh muscles to quiver, and she grimaced.

"That's it, Trish," Craig encouraged, his voice filled with genuine support. "You're doing great. I know it's tough, but keep going. You're stronger than you think."

Trish nodded, determination etched on her face. She continued to bend and straighten her knee, each repetition bringing her closer to regaining her strength. As she flexed her calf, a tightness coursed through her leg, causing her to pause.

"Is everything okay?" Craig asked, watching her closely.

She nodded, a bead of sweat forming on her brow. "It's just a bit tight."

Craig nodded in understanding. "Keep pushing through that tightness. You'll get there."

Trish took a deep breath and resumed the exercises, pushing herself to go beyond her comfort zone. With each repetition, the discomfort lessened, and a glimmer of hope emerged.

"I can feel it getting easier," she announced, a hint of excitement in her voice.

Craig nodded; his eyes filled with pride. "That's the spirit, Trish! Your hard work is paying off. Just a little bit more, and we'll be done for today."

Trish mustered her remaining strength and completed the final set of exercises. As she finished, a sense of accomplishment washed over her.

"You did great today, Trish," Craig cheered. He set down his own weights and walked over to her, his eyes reflecting a steadfast determination. "Every small step you take is a victory. If you continue to push past the doubt and discomfort like you did today, I can guarantee you will be walking freely in no time," he spoke with conviction.

Trish wiped the sweat from her brow with the back of her hand, pausing for a moment to catch her breath. "You're right, Craig," she admitted, her voice laced with a mixture of weariness and determination. "But sometimes all I feel is a strong desire to just throw in the towel."

Craig's face softened, his eyes filled with empathy. He reached out and gently placed a hand on her shoulder, offering a reassuring squeeze. "I understand. We all have moments when we feel like giving up. But you've come so far already. Remember why you started this journey in the first place. I can't say it enough. You're stronger than you think, Trish."

"Thanks." She smiled gratefully.

Craig returned the smile. She left then and headed to the changing room to change out of her sweaty clothes. Then, she headed to the front of the clinic to wait for Nikki. The lavender dress she wore fluttered in the gentle breeze, even as she welcomed the warmth of the afternoon sun on her skin. She looked heavenward. At the sound of an engine, her head came down just in time to see her sister's car pull up to the curb and stop. She drew in a deep, steadying breath before slowly making her way over to the car.

As she approached the car, her eyes flickered with a mix of anticipation and anxiety. The mere thought of sitting inside a vehicle ever since the accident sent shivers down her spine every time. It was a reminder of the night that had shattered her life into fragments. With a deep breath, she opened the door and slid onto the plush leather seat, her fingers lightly tracing the intricate patterns etched into the upholstery.

"Hey, Sis," Nikki greeted. "How was your session today?" she asked as she pulled off.

Trish's gaze remained fixed on the passing scenery outside the window, her knuckles turning white as she clenched the edge of her seat. "It was all right," she replied, her voice tinged with a hint of apprehension.

Nikki's eyes sparkled with determination as she leaned back against her seat and glanced at Trish, her voice filled with warmth. "You're doing amazing, you know. I'm proud of you, Trish. You've come so far since the accident and waking up."

Trish lifted her head to offer her sister a tight smile before her attention was back on her hands, now tightly curled in her lap.

"So...how's it going with Reed? Any progress there?"

Trish's breath hitched, a mix of emotions swirling within her. Reed had always been an enigmatic presence in her life and had been a constant source of support throughout her recovery. "Oh, Reed," she murmured, her lips curling into a wistful smile. "We're still just friends. Nothing more, really."

"Come on, Trish. You deserve a little romance after everything you've been through. Maybe it's time to let love find its way back into your life." Nikki's voice was laced with playful encouragement.

Trish's gaze shifted, her eyes meeting Nikki's in a moment of silent understanding. "I don't know, Nikki. It's just... hard to trust again. After what happened in my first marriage."

"You never told me what happened with you and Derek," Nikki said, her eyes questioning.

A memory flashed through Trish's mind, causing an involuntary shudder. "It was a long time ago and best left in the past," she sighed. She could see the question in her sister's eyes, but this was one story she was not ready to open up about to anyone.

Nikki's hand reached out and gently touched Trish's leg. "I understand, Sis. But remember, love has a funny way of healing even the deepest wounds. Just stay open to the possibility. You never know what might happen."

Trish's lips curved into a small smile, gratitude shining in her eyes. "Thanks, Nikki. Lately, you always know how to make me feel better." A chuckle slipped through her lips. Nikki grinned.

"We're home. Safe and sound," Nikki announced.

Trish's eyes widened in surprise before looking through the windshield to see that they were, in fact, back at the house. She released a sigh of relief as she unfurled her hands, and her shoulders slackened.

Nikki was the first one out of the car, and she quickly came to the passenger side to help Trish out.

"You don't have to help me, you know. I can do it by myself."

Nikki gave her an apologetic look before stepping back, giving her room to exit the car. She then proceeded to walk behind her as they made their way up the porch steps.

"Amy made a Bundt cake this morning before she left for her classes. Do you want me to cut you a slice and pour you some milk?" Nikki offered as they stepped into the foyer.

"Yeah. I would," Trish accepted.

Nikki nodded and headed for the kitchen, and Trish followed. Hoisting herself onto the high chair by the kitchen island, she watched as Nikki cut two healthy slices of the cake and placed them onto the plates before pouring two glasses of milk to go with them.

"Thanks," Trish accepted when her sister slid the plate over to her. Using the fork to spear a piece of the sweet confection, she brought it to her lips and tasted it. The moment cake touched her tongue, Trish moaned with satisfaction.

"This is so good," she complimented. "Amy is so talented."

"Isn't she?" Nikki's lips curved up, and her eyes shone

with pride. Trish's heart constricted at this. "I told her she could literally open her bakery now, and I would be one of her first and most loyal customers, and of course, she would have so many other loyal customers she wouldn't know where to put them."

"How nice," Trish said with a facsimile of a smile as she stared into the glass of milk.

"Please don't do that, Trish," Nikki pleaded.

"Do what?" Trish asked, raising her head so her eyes met Nikki's.

"Exactly this," Nikki responded, her voice a gentle caress laden with the weight of understanding. "You're scrutinizing your bond with Amy, contrasting it with ours. Amy yearns for your love, Trish. She craves the warmth of a mother's touch. And yet, you've been a fortress of emotional walls. This cold detachment, where you refuse to explain to her what happened all those years ago, it reflects onto her, making her hesitant in seeking your affection. The real tragedy is, Trish, that you're denying yourself the chance to deepen your bond with your own daughter."

A bitter chuckle escaped Trish's lips, a hollow sound that echoed around the room. "Of course, of course, it's all on me, isn't it?" She pressed her palms flat onto the cool marble of the island counter, her knuckles white. "I was the one who abandoned her to the mercy of strangers. I allowed her to fall into the hands of people who turned a blind eye to her safety. And now, I'm the one sabotaging the possibility of mending the wounds, of forming an authentic connection with her. God, I truly believed I had evolved beyond being such a colossal failure."

A torrent of hot tears broke free, coursing down her cheeks, mirroring the tumultuous storm of guilt and regret raging within her. "Trish," Nikki began, her voice a comforting whisper against the cacophony of Trish's self-reproach.

"No, Nikki," Trish interrupted, her voice sharp with a desperate resolve. "I can't... I can't face this right now. I... I need to be alone." With a trembling hand, she lifted the glass of milk, draining its contents in one swift motion before shoving back from the counter with a harsh scrape of chair legs against the floor.

The room seemed to hold its breath as Trish, over-whelmed with despair, trudged out of the kitchen, her footsteps echoing with the weight of her remorse. Nikki was left behind, her expression a mirror of helplessness, watching the retreating figure of her sister.

Chapter Six

"**I** knew you would fail the moment you decided to look for your daughter, Trish. Because that's all you know how to do—be a failure and disappointment to this family."

Trish's eyes shot open, her heart pounding against her chest as the remnants of her dream clung to her senses. The room seemed darker, the air heavier, as if the weight of her father's words still lingered around her.

A shiver crawled up her spine as she recalled the haunting echo of his voice, dripping with disdain and disappointment. It was a voice she thought she had escaped, buried beneath years of resilience and determination. Yet, in the depths of her subconscious, it clawed its way back to torment her once more.

She sat up in bed, her hands trembling, and the moonlight filtering through the curtains cast eerie shadows across her face. The room held an uncanny stillness. Looking over at the bedside table, she realized it was still night, just a little after one.

Releasing a heavy breath, she scooted to the edge of

the bed and carefully got up. Her leg felt stiff, and as she stood to her feet, she almost toppled over but quickly grabbed onto the edge of the bedside table for support.

When she felt relaxed enough, she made her way to the kitchen. Digging through the freezer, she secured the tub of chocolate ice cream. Grabbing a spoon, she sat by the island and began digging into the sweet, creamy delight to drown her sorrows.

At the sound of footsteps, Trish's head swiveled to the door just as Amy walked into the kitchen.

"I couldn't sleep," Amy answered her unasked question.

"Join me," Trish invited, holding up the tub of ice cream. Without a word, Amy went to the kitchen counter and removed a spoon from one of the drawers. She then walked back over to the island and sat across from her mother. Trish placed the tub on the island between them. Together, they silently at their ice cream.

The rhythmic scrape of spoons against the bowls continued, the sound serving as a backdrop to the unspoken dialogue between mother and daughter. Trish's heart pounded with anticipation, knowing the moment to open up about her past had arrived.

"I'm not sure how much Nikki told you about the past and our parents..." A flicker of vulnerability danced across her eyes before she met Amy's gaze. "Our father was an upstanding member of his community, and he had been strict with Nikki and me because we could not be anything less than perfect for him."

Trish took a deep breath, her fingers tightening around the spoon. "He wanted us, his two daughters, to follow in his footsteps, to carry on his legacy, so when I got pregnant at nineteen, he was not happy."

Amy's spoon clinked against the bowl as her grip tightened imperceptibly.

"He demanded I give you up to preserve his carefully crafted image."

Amy's eyes darkened, but no words left her lips.

Trish's gaze focused on the swirling patterns of the ice cream. "I was young, naïve, and trapped in the web he had spun around us. I didn't have many choices to make for myself, but I knew deep down I couldn't bring a child into an environment like that. So, I made the agonizing decision to give you up for adoption."

Amy's spoon clattered against the counter as she pushed herself away from the island, her eyes glistening with pain. "Thank you for telling me the truth, Mom. But it doesn't change the fact you didn't want me then, or else you wouldn't have given me away."

Trish's heart ached at the anguish in Amy's voice. "Amy, that's not true." She reached out, her hand hovering in the empty space between them, but Amy turned away, her shoulders weighed down by the burden of her own emotions.

"I get that you were young, believe me. But how can you say it's not true when you waited all these years before coming to find me?"

Silence settled once again, thick and heavy, before Amy left the kitchen, her steps echoing down the hallway. Trish remained where she was as tears rolled down her face.

The next morning, Trish stood behind the front desk of the inn. Her eyes sparkled with a mixture of joy and determination. "We're very happy to have you staying with us, Mr. and Mrs. Smith," she greeted the couple as she handed them the key to their room.

"Thank you, Trish. We're very happy to be here. We can't wait to explore this beautiful town," the woman who looked to be in her early sixties replied.

"I would be happy to provide suggestions if you're not sure where you would like to visit," Trish offered with an inviting smile.

"That's kind of you, but we have our itinerary all planned out," the man spoke up this time.

"All right. Well, I hope you'll have fun because Camano has so much to offer," Trish said, walking from behind the desk. Dorothy will see you to your room, she gestured to the woman standing by the set of stairs leading to the first floor.

"Thank you for all your help. We appreciate it," Mrs. Smith smiled.

"It was my pleasure," Trish genuinely responded. She watched as Dorothy led them up the steps to their room.

Just then, another couple entered the lobby, their faces beaming with the glow of newlywed bliss. Trish's eyes lit up as she greeted them warmly, her voice infused with genuine excitement. "Welcome to our little piece of paradise! I'm Trish, the proud owner of this charming inn. You must be the Reids."

"Yes, we are," the man replied proudly, then turned to look at his wife affectionately. The woman blushed profusely as her lips turned up in a sweet smile directed at him. Trish smiled too, admiring their seeming devotion to each other.

"You've chosen a wonderful place to celebrate your honeymoon. Camano Island is simply enchanting," she expressed.

The couple exchanged a glance, their smiles widening. The woman, her eyes sparkling like the azure sea, spoke up, "Thank you, Trish. We've heard such wonderful things about this place. We're here to immerse ourselves in the island's beauty and make memories to last a lifetime."

Trish nodded; her eyes filled with understanding. "You've come to the right place, my dear. Camano is a treasure trove of natural wonders and hidden gems. Your stay here will be nothing short of magical."

She handed them the keys to their room. "Thank you," the woman said.

"You're most welcome. Let me see you to your room," Trish offered when she didn't see Dorothy returning. With a slight wince, she led them up the stairs. She couldn't stop the slight hiss that whistled through her lips as the strain on her healing leg increased.

"Are you all right?" the woman asked, her voice rolling with concern.

"I am. My leg just has a little cramp from sitting too long." She brushed off their concerned glances with a reassuring smile, despite the twinge of pain that shot through her. Worry remained on their faces.

"Please don't worry about me," Trish reassured them, her voice laced with determination. "This little inconvenience won't stop me from taking care of my guests."

Once they reached the door of their junior room, Trish wished them a great rest of their day, her heart swelling with a mix of satisfaction and concern. As she returned downstairs, she couldn't hide the grimace that flickered across her face, a silent acknowledgment of the pain she felt.

Kaylyn walked through the front door just then. A frown transformed her face as she watched Trish descend the steps. "Trish, you need to take it easy," she scolded, her voice filled with genuine concern. "Enough of this stubbornness. You're heading straight to your office."

Reluctantly, Trish followed Kaylyn's firm instruction, limping her way to the cozy sanctuary of her office. Moments later, Kaylyn appeared, holding a tray laden with painkillers, a mouthwatering spread from the adjoining Lot 28, and a refreshing glass of water.

"Sit down," Kaylyn commanded gently, placing the tray before Trish. You've done more than enough for today. Let me take care of the rest. Dorothy will see to the new guests.

"Thanks, Kaylyn," Trish replied with a grateful smile.

"You need to stop working yourself to the bone whenever there is a problem you're struggling with," Kaylyn spoke, her voice full of wisdom.

Trish's eyes widened in surprise.

"I know you, remember?" Kaylyn raised an eyebrow.

Trish's lips turned up in a smile. "Okay. I'll take it easy. Thanks for this," she gestured to the food and painkillers.

"It was my pleasure," Kaylyn smiled at her. "Relax. I mean it." She narrowed her eyes in warning.

Trish chuckled as the little woman left her office. She then dove into the food. Her stomach rumbled in appreciation. She hadn't realized she was that hungry. But then again, the only thing she had consumed was the ice cream with Amy, and that was hours ago. In record time, she was finished. She took the painkillers and prepared to take a nap. The knock on the door interrupted her plans. "Come in," she called out.

The door opened, and Reed walked in, a faint smile tugging at the corners of his lips. "Hi, Trish. How are you?"

"Reed? This is a surprise," Trish responded, a mix of genuine surprise and delight coloring her voice. Her heart skipped a beat as she took in his familiar face and his warm gray eyes that were trained on her.

"I stopped by the house, but Nikki told me you were here. I hope I didn't catch you at a bad time."

"No, not at all," Trish assured him.

"Could I steal a moment of your time? There's something I'd like to discuss with you," he said, his voice laced with a mix of anticipation and vulnerability.

Caught off guard, Trish hesitated for a brief moment before nodding, curiosity mingling with a hint of angst. "Of course, Reed."

"Let's go for a walk. It's a beautiful afternoon," he suggested.

They strolled along the winding path that meandered through a picturesque garden, the vibrant colors of fully bloomed flowers serving as a backdrop to their conversation. The air hummed with the songs of birds, lending a touch of serenity to the atmosphere.

As they walked side by side, Reed's voice trembled with emotion. "Trish, I want to tell you something. When I found out about your accident, I was devastated. The thought of losing you, losing the light you bring to the world... It was unbearable. But when you woke up from that coma, it was like a beacon of hope in the darkness. You're a remarkable woman, Trish, and I've come to cherish not only your incredible work at the Humane Society but also the friendship we've cultivated over the years."

A flicker of realization sparked in Trish's eyes. She could see the truth etched in Reed's words, the unspoken confession that lingered between them. Her heart swelled with a mixture of joy and apprehension, for she knew the weight of her response.

"Reed," she began, her voice soft and tinged with regret. "I can't deny the deep connection we share, and I'm grateful for your presence in my life. I think I know what it is you want to tell me... but right now, my focus needs to be on repairing the fragile relationship I have with Amy."

The sting from her daughter's words this morning was still fresh in her mind. "She is my number one priority right, and I can't think of pursuing anything outside of that now."

She could see the disappointment shadowing Reed's face, mirroring the disappointment that welled up within her own heart. The vulnerability in his eyes made her ache, but she knew she had to remain resolute in her decision.

Reed's expression softened, and he reached out to gently touch her arm. "Trish, I respect your choice. Your relationship with Amy is important, and I understand that. I'll always be here for you, no matter what. You're an incredible woman, and I cherish every moment we've shared."

A bittersweet smile curved Trish's lips, gratitude and regret intermingling as she looked into Reed's eyes. They stood there for a moment, the weight of unspoken words hanging in the air, and then she nodded, silently acknowledging the depth of his understanding.

Chapter Seven

Amy sat at her workstation, her heart racing with a mixture of excitement and nerves. As the female culinary students eagerly awaited the arrival of the new guest lecturer, whispers of anticipation filled the air. Rumors had been circulating about the so-called "cute" and "hot" chef who was about to grace their classroom.

She turned around when Professor Reynolds cleared his throat. "Ladies and gentlemen, may I have your attention, please? Today, we are honored to have a very special guest with us. A true prodigy in the world of pastry arts," he announced, his voice booming through the room. He paused for effect as everyone waited for him to finish.

"Please welcome Gabriel Blanchet!"

The room erupted into polite applause as Gabriel entered, a subtle smile playing on his lips. Amy's eyes widened in recognition, and a gasp escaped her lips. It was the guy she'd met in the culinary store.

"Wow. He's quite the looker, right?" Jill whispered, nudging her with her elbow.

Amy's cheeks flushed, her gaze reluctantly drifting toward her friend. "Yeah, he's... handsome, I guess," she replied, trying to keep her voice casual.

"Don't give me that, Amy. At least look at him," Jill said, pointing her chin toward the front of the class.

Her eyes lifted to find Gabriel's green eyes focused on her, his expression unreadable. Her heart beat erratically against her chest. She couldn't deny the magnetic pull he had on her.

"I can practically see the stars in your eyes." Amy shook her head, breaking the moment that passed between them. "Admit it. You've got a little crush on him!" Jill teased, a mischievous grin on her lips.

Amy rolled her eyes, her lips curling into a half-hearted smile. "Okay, fine. Maybe I find him attractive. But looks aren't everything, you know. Besides, charm and talent are two different things."

Jill chuckled, her eyes twinkling with amusement. "Well, let's see if he lives up to the hype. Maybe he'll surprise us all."

As if on cue, Gabriel began his introduction, his voice smooth and velvety, commanding the attention of everyone in the room. "Thank you, Chef Reynolds, for the warm welcome. It's an honor to be here today amongst such talented individuals. Today, I will be sharing with you my secrets to creating exquisite pastries that transcend mere desserts. I believe that in every bite lies the power to transport someone to a world of pure bliss."

Amy couldn't help but be intrigued. She had to admit Gabriel spoke with eloquence, his words weaving a tantalizing web of culinary artistry and bellying a knowledge and passion for one's craft.

She watched as he effortlessly demonstrated the delicate technique of tempering chocolate. It was such a simple technique, but the way his fingers moved was with grace and precision.

Impressed, Amy leaned toward Jill and whispered, "Okay, I have to admit, he's got skills. Maybe there's more to him than meets the eye."

Jill winked, her eyes twinkling with mischief. "You see? Looks, talent, and charm all in one package. Who could resist?"

Amy smiled nervously and averted her gaze. Who could resist? She had been thinking about their encounter in the store two days ago and had hoped she'd run into him somewhere around town. She didn't expect it would be at her school and he would be her lecturer at that.

"And this is one of our promising students, Amy Parker." Amy's chest tightened as her heart beat wickedly against her chest.

Chef Reynolds and Gabriel were standing at her workstation.

"Amy," Gabriel spoke her name, his voice sliding over the word as if it was the first time he was saying it.

"Good afternoon, Chef Blanchet. It is a pleasure to meet you," Amy rushed out nervously, bowing slightly.

"Likewise, Amy. And please, Gabriel is fine," he responded, his eyes glinting. "I look forward to seeing what you can do." With that, he walked away, leaving Amy dumbfounded, trying to decipher what that interaction was. She put it out of her head, prepared to do her best and not be distracted. As Gabriel instructed them to go about crafting their pastry pieces, Amy became lost in her work because, for her... it too was her passion.

However, as he went around the room, providing feedback and guidance, Amy noticed a distinct change in his demeanor when he reached her workstation. His charming smile seemed to fade, replaced by a critical gaze that made her stomach twist with unease.

"What do we have here?" Gabriel asked, his tone laced with condescension. "Is this supposed to be a pastry, Amy? I must say, it looks more like a misshapen lump of dough than anything remotely edible." He released the pastry like it was indeed a lump of clay.

Amy's face flushed with embarrassment, and she felt her confidence crumble beneath Gabriel's cutting words. Her classmates exchanged uncomfortable glances; their sympathy evident. But Gabriel seemed to relish in his power to humiliate her. Amy stared at him, betrayed. How could she have thought this man was a kind person? All illusions she'd had of him instantly disappeared.

"That was harsh," Jill whispered, bewildered when Gabriel walked off.

"Yeah," Amy said simply, watching as Gabriel patiently talked with another student, giving him pointers on what he could do next time to improve the consistency of the pastry he made.

"It feels personal," Jill continued. "Like he knows you or something." Amy ignored her and turned to her station, preparing to make her next set of pastries. She worked hard on it, ignoring the doubts that had seeped in like a sore from his words earlier.

When he returned to her station, her back stiffened, her eyes guarded, hiding the fear she felt as she waited for him to talk.

"You call this a pastry?" Gabriel's voice dripped with disdain as he held up her raspberry tart. "It's uneven, the crust is overbaked, and the filling lacks any semblance of flavor. Honestly, I expected more from you, Amy.

Amy's heart sank as the entire class witnessed her humiliation once more. She felt the weight of Gabriel's words pressing down on her, suffocating her dreams. Anger surged through her veins, and she clenched her fists, fighting back the tears.

"Is there something wrong with my work or just me?" Her voice quivered with a mix of hurt and defiance. "Because it seems like you're going out of your way to make me look and feel incompetent."

Gabriel's eyes narrowed, a flicker of surprise crossing his face. "You think this is personal? I'm simply here to critique your skills honestly. If you can't handle it, maybe you should reconsider your career choice."

Amy felt her confidence shatter, her mind echoing the haunting words of her adoptive father. She had spent her life trying to prove him wrong, to prove she was capable of achieving greatness. Yet, at this moment, it felt like all her efforts were in vain.

Jill rushed to her side as she walked out of the kitchen, her voice filled with concern. "Amy, don't let him get to you. You're talented, and you have the potential to be an incredible pastry chef. You're one of the best students in class. You deserve to be here," she encouraged.

But Amy could barely hear Jill's words over the deafening doubts in her mind. Gabriel's constant criticism had made her question everything she had worked for. It was as if he had singled her out, determined to crush her spirit and prove her adoptive father right. What happened to the kind stranger she'd met in that store?

As she sat in her car, the weight of Gabriel's insults bore down on her, threatening to crush her spirit entirely. Amy fought back tears; her heart heavy with self-doubt. But deep within her, a flicker of resilience remained, a determination to rise above the chaos and prove herself worthy.

However, as the days went by, Gabriel's relentless criticism of Amy's work intensified, leaving her feeling targeted and disheartened. She couldn't understand why he seemed to harbor such animosity toward her. Had she done something to insult him back at the Plaza? Or was he simply a jerk who enjoyed making others feel small?

* * *

Amy stepped into the cozy coffee shop on Sunset Boulevard, the scent of freshly brewed coffee wafting through the air. The warm autumn sun filtered through the large windows, casting a gentle glow on the patrons huddled over their laptops or engrossed in conversation. She approached the counter, her gaze drifting over the chalkboard menu, and the barista, a young woman with a friendly smile, caught her attention.

"Hey there! Can I help you with something?" the barista asked, her voice bubbling with enthusiasm.

Amy hesitated for a moment before responding, her eyes fixed on the pumpkin spice latte listed on the menu. "Um, yeah, I'll have a pumpkin spice latte, please," she said, her voice tinged with weariness.

The barista nodded, her hands deftly working the espresso machine. "Great choice! It's perfect for the season," she replied, her tone filled with warmth.

"Thank you," Amy smiled, accepting the steaming cup. The aroma of spices enveloped her senses as she made her way to a corner booth. She sank into the plush seat, wrapping her hands around the cup, seeking solace in its comforting warmth. As she sipped the rich, creamy beverage, her thoughts drifted to Gabriel.

She couldn't shake off the pain of his cruel words. She tried to block the negative thoughts, but it only lasted a few seconds as she sipped her latte before it flitted to the conversation she'd had with Trish over a week ago.

The question that had been haunting her echoed in her mind, and she couldn't help but feel a pang of hurt and confusion. Why hadn't Trish looked for her all those years if she truly loved her? It made her question the depth of her mother's affection, threatening to shatter the fragile trust she so desperately wanted to hold on to.

"Hello, Amy."

Amy lifted her gaze to the old woman standing at her table with a bright smile on her wrinkled face.

"Hello," Amy replied hesitantly, trying to remember where she knew her from.

"You don't seem to remember me, but then again, we've met briefly once at your mother's welcome home party. I'm Nelly," the woman explained.

"Hi, Miss Nelly. I remember you now," Amy replied with a soft smile as she recalled she had indeed met her that time, and she'd also seen her a few times after that. Amy subtly scanned the café and realized all the booths were full. "Would you like to have a seat?" she offered.

"Well, don't mind if I do. I need to rest more than I used to. These old bones aren't as strong as back in the day," Nelly chuckled, gently sliding into the seat opposite Amy. "Now, my dear, what's got you wearing such a frown?" she asked, her voice carrying a hint of mischief.

Amy looked up, her eyes meeting Nelly's. She managed a weak smile, but her weariness betrayed her.

"It's nothing, Ms. Nelly. Just some things on my mind, that's all."

"You know, my dear, sometimes it helps to share your troubles. Talking about them can lighten the burden," Nelly said, her voice filled with wisdom. 'And please, call me Nelly."

Amy sighed; her gaze fixed on the tabletop. "I'm just having some problems with someone at school who hasn't been very nice to me," she revealed, her voice laced with frustration.

"Ah...I see." Nelly leaned closer; her voice gentle yet firm. "Let me give you a piece of advice, my dear. The opinions of others do not define your worth. Don't let hurtful people take up space in that pretty little head of yours. I can tell you are a very bright young woman, and you are destined to go places, so rise above the negativity and keep showing them what you're made of."

Amy nodded, her eyes meeting Nelly's with gratitude. "Thank you, Nelly. It means a lot to hear that."

"You're welcome, my dear," Nelly smiled, her eyes shining with kindness.

Amy's lips lifted into a smile.

Chapter Eight

"Good morning, class. Today, we continue to explore the art of pastry-making. Precision, attention to detail, and a discerning palate are what set apart the amateurs from the masters." Gabriel's voice, smooth as caramel, pierced the silence of the kitchen as the students stood at their workstations waiting for instructions.

Gabriel's green gaze landed on Amy for a brief second, but it was enough to accelerate her heartbeat. The past week had been a relentless onslaught of criticism from Gabriel, but after her conversation with Nelly, she was trying her best to weather the storm as she worked hard to prove him wrong. But there were days when she still questioned her own abilities.

"Today, we will be making macarons," he continued, unaware of the anxiety he'd triggered by just his mere presence in the kitchen. "The ingredients are simple: almond flour, egg whites, and powdered sugar. I expect you to follow the recipe." He paused for half a minute as the students waited for further instructions. "Begin."

"Yes, Chef," the class chorused.

Amy got to work immediately, ensuring that she used the right measurements and folding the ingredients until the batter was airy. She then piped them onto the baking sheets in small, round shapes before leaving them to rest to work on the filling she would be using. She placed the baking sheets into the oven and set the timer.

A satisfied smile graced her lips when she removed the macarons from the oven. They had a crisp outer shell that glistened.

"Wow, Amy. Those look great," Jill complimented as she came to stand beside her.

"They're okay, I guess," Amy replied with a shrug of her shoulders.

"Are you kidding me?" Jill asked with an incredulous stare. "Yours are by far the best I've seen." Amy smiled appreciatively this time. "There is no way that Gabriel won't be impressed this time."

And just like that, her anxiety returned.

"Let me get on this filling for my macarons. They look more like buns, but what can I do?" Amy gave her friend a sympathetic look before turning to finish up her presentation.

Half an hour later, Gabriel's voice rang out. "Okay, ladies and gents, it's time to unveil your work." With that, he started walking to the students' stations.

"This could have been done better, Jill, but I see the potential, and I'm sure you'll do better next time.

"Yes, Chef," Jill replied with a slight bow of her head.

He turned to Amy just then, and her heart sank as she glanced at her workstation, where her meticulously piped macarons sat in neat rows. Her hands trembled slightly, betraying the mix of frustration and self-doubt coursing through her veins.

"What are these?" he asked, lifting a macaron from the tray. His eyes squinted in confusion as if it was the first time he had ever seen anything like the pastry he held.

"Um. They're macarons, Chef," Amy responded, her voice quivering with uncertainty.

"They look more like hockey pucks than delicate pastries," he responded with a frown before placing the macaron he held on top of the pyramid she had made from the pastries. "This is what happens when you take the unconventional route and do not follow simple instructions and measurements," he said loud enough for the other students, whose eyes were already trained on the pair.

A few students snickered at Gabriel's remark, and Amy fought the urge to snap back at him. Taking a deep breath, determined to maintain her composure, she responded, "I followed the recipe precisely, Chef Gabriel." Her voice steady despite the unease swirling within her. "I even double-checked the measurements."

"Are you sure you used the correct measuring cups, piped the batter as was instructed, and let them rest out for the prescribed amount of time?" he questioned.

Amy swallowed hard, stumped by his questions. She was certain she had followed the recipe through and through, and yet here was Gabriel questioning her capabilities when, for the most part, all she had seen him do was commend her classmates and encourage them to do better next time.

"I did everything by the book, Chef. I am certain I did not skip a step." Her voice came out timid and unsure.

Gabriel's emerald eyes stared at her for a long time before he said anything else, and she, like the rest of the class, waited with bated breath. He held the macaron to his lips and took a small bite.

"This," Gabriel said, his voice stern, "needs more work. The texture is all wrong, and the flavors clash like a cacophony of discordant notes. It's clear you haven't put in the effort to truly understand your ingredients."

Amy's face burned with embarrassment as the snickers of her classmates filled the air. She bit her tongue, fighting the urge to retort. His words were like serrated knives slicing into her confidence.

"You have to feel the passion for what you are doing for it to come out the way it should, Amy."

"Thank you for your feedback, Gabriel," she replied, her voice laced with forced calmness. "I'll take your suggestions into consideration."

Gabriel's gaze softened, as did his voice. "Consideration won't be enough, Amy. You must learn to embrace precision and discipline if you want to succeed in this industry. Otherwise, you'll forever be an amateur in a sea of professionals."

Amy wasn't sure why he was looking at her like that, but she was sure she did not want his pity, not after the way he had just embarrassed her in front of the whole class. She simply nodded in response and then averted her gaze, hoping he would leave her alone now.

After a pause that seemed like minutes instead of seconds, Gabriel moved on. She released a heavy breath.

As soon as the class was over and she had cleaned her workstation, Amy quickly left the kitchen.

"Amy! Wait up!"

She looked over her shoulder to see Jill walking in her

direction. She slowed down until she came to a stop and waited on her friend.

"You okay?" Jill asked the moment she fell into step with Amy.

"Define okay," Amy muttered, her head down.

"Amy, don't take it personally. Gabriel is critical of everyone. He's just pushing us to our limits so we can grow."

Amy shook her head, her voice edged with frustration. "No, Jill. It's not the same. It feels like he's singling me out, as if he's determined to make me doubt myself. I used to believe in my skills, but now... now I question everything."

Jill's eyes softened with empathy as she reached out to touch Amy's arm. "Remember why you started, Amy. Remember the passion that brought you here. Gabriel's criticism may sting, but it's not a reflection of your abilities. You're awesome, girl."

"Thanks, Jill. I appreciate it, but right now, I feel anything but awesome," she replied. "I'll see you in class. There's something I need to do first," she expressed before finding herself walking down the corridor that led to Professor Reynolds's office. She took a deep breath before knocking on the door. She was nervous about confronting her professor, but she couldn't shake off her dissatisfaction with Gabriel.

"Come in," Professor Reynolds called out, his voice warm and inviting.

Amy pushed open the door and stepped into the cozy office decorated with shelves of culinary books and framed certificates. Professor Reynolds looked up from his desk, adjusting his glasses.

"Amy, what brings you here today?" he asked,

gesturing for her to take a seat.

Amy hesitated for a moment before speaking. "Professor Reynolds, I wanted to discuss something that has been bothering me. It's about the guest lecturer, Gabriel."

Professor Reynolds leaned back in his chair, a curious expression on his face. "Gabriel? What seems to be the issue?"

Amy bit her lip, collecting her thoughts. "Well, Professor, I have to be honest. I don't think Gabriel's teaching methods are effective. I feel like I'm not learning as much as possible, and his approach just doesn't resonate with me."

Professor Reynolds nodded; his expression thoughtful. "I understand your concerns, Amy. But let me assure you, Gabriel is an excellent pastry chef—one of the best in his field. Although he's young, he has a wealth of experience and knowledge to share. His techniques might be different from what you're used to, but they can help you hone your skills in ways you might not expect."

Amy's brows furrowed in frustration. "I understand that, but..." she sighed, her shoulders deflated. She looked up at her professor with vulnerability. "It feels like nothing I have done so far is good enough. He questions my techniques and my motivation. At this point, I'm beginning to question if I even belong here," she confessed, fighting the tears threatening to fall.

Professor Reynolds leaned forward; his voice gentle yet firm. "Amy, being a good teacher is not solely about following a tried-and-true method. It's about challenging your students, pushing them out of their comfort zones, and encouraging them to explore different approaches. Gabriel is trying to do just that. He wants you to think critically and expand your skill set."

Amy's frustration grew, and she couldn't help but feel a pang of disappointment. She had hoped that Professor Reynolds would understand her concerns and support her.

"But, Professor, I thought you would be on my side," she blurted, her voice tinged with disappointment as a tear finally escaped and slid down her cheek. "I wanted to come to you because I trust your judgment, not to be told I should just accept Gabriel's approach." Her eyes widened in surprise that she had just spoken to him like that.

Professor Reynolds sighed, his expression softening. "Amy, I appreciate your trust in me, and I understand your frustration. But if you're truly concerned about Gabriel's approach, I encourage you to talk to him directly. Share your thoughts, ask him questions, and express your concerns. Open communication is vital in any learning environment, and it's through dialogue that we can find common ground and grow together. I want all of my students to excel and to become all that they can be, and I believe that Gabriel is able to bring that out in you. If he didn't see the potential for something great, he wouldn't be pushing you this hard. Talk to him," he encouraged.

Amy wiped the errant tear and nodded. "You're right, Professor. I'll speak to Gabriel," she agreed before grabbing up her bag and leaving his office. As soon as the door shut behind her, her back slumped against it in dejection.

When she was calm enough to leave, she made her way down the corridor, trying to get to her theory class. As she turned the corner, her path collided with Seline, one of her classmates.

"Well, if it isn't Miss I'm the Greatest Culinary

Student. Good thing Chef Gabriel is here to cut you down a peg or two," Seline sneered, her words dripping with venom. Two of her friends, who were just a few steps behind her, snickered.

"What do you want, Seline?" Amy asked with a frustrated breath.

"Oh, nothing. I'm just glad someone is finally seeing how overrated you are. There's only one top chef in class, and that's gonna be me," she said, patting her chest.

"Look, Seline, I don't have time for this. I have a class, and you're clearly a delusional, mean girl, so excuse me." With that, Amy sidestepped her to continue walking.

"I heard she was adopted," one of Seline's friends whispered, her voice dripping with disdain. "Her real mother just now chose to rescue her from a life of squalor."

Amy's steps faltered, her heart pounding in her chest. The words sliced through her like a knife, reopening the wound of her past. She hadn't known she was adopted, and while she had come to terms with it, the cruel remarks still stung.

"How pathetic," Seline called after her, the taunting words fueling Amy's anguish. She bypassed her class and headed for the exit.

Reaching her car, Amy collapsed against the driver's seat, her tears flowing freely. Doubts and insecurities flooded her thoughts, and she questioned whether she truly belonged in this place, in this quest for connection with a birth mother who didn't want her all those years ago and never came looking until now.

As the tears streamed down her face, Amy allowed herself a moment of vulnerability and heartbreak.

Chapter Nine

"Just fill out here, here, and...here." Trish pointed out the parts on the form to the couple standing before her with a bright-faced little girl, not more than five.

Underneath the fluttering paper banner that read, "Adopt a Pet Today," Trish was ensconced in the flurry of the event, hosted amidst the natural splendor of the seven-acre Henry Hollow Off-Leash Dog Park on Camano Island. Surrounded by towering evergreens and sprawling meadows, the park had been magically transformed into a beautiful haven for animals and their admirers.

"Thank you," Moira, the mom, smiled before taking a pen from her handbag and leaning over to write on the form.

"So, Hailey, I can already tell you're going to be very good to Charlie over there." She threw a glance over her shoulder at the Jack Russell terrier in the enclosed space looking up at them, his little tail wagging as if he knew what was happening. She turned her attention to the little girl, who was now bobbing her head in eager agreement.

'We're going to be best friends, and I'm going to love him forever and ever," Hailey spoke, her voice bubbling with excitement and conviction.

The adults chuckled at her enthusiasm.

"What now?" Moira asked after handing the form back to Trish.

Trish did a quick scan and noted the responses. Her lips curved into a satisfied grin. "Come tomorrow, a member of the society will be by your home to do a check, and if all goes well, you will be the proud new family of Charlie over there," she informed them.

"Great," the father spoke up with a satisfied grin of his own, while Hailey bounded up and down with a wide smile.

"Thank you so much for your help, Trish. It was truly great of you to help us," Moira spoke gratefully.

"It was my pleasure," Trish replied. The smile remained on her lips as she watched the family walk away.

As the sun swelled high above the emerald canopy, casting a golden glow upon the scene, the air brimmed with anticipation and joy. The park's verdant expanse was now a vibrant tableau, alive with wagging tails, purring kittens, and the tender hopes of compassionate humans. It was a day of boundless promise, and for these innocent creatures, it was a journey to find their forever homes amidst the enchanting embrace of Henry Hollow.

A few feet away, Reed directed the volunteers with practiced ease. There was an unmistakable tension between them, a delicate dance of words left unspoken and feelings left unexpressed. A week had passed since he had been on the verge of baring his heart to her, but she had stopped him, her own heart quivering with trepidation. Between her new and developing relationship with Amy and her own insecurities, Trish felt like she was trying to navigate a stormy sea without a compass.

"Trish." Reed's voice pulled her from her thoughts. "Could you help me with the new arrivals?"

"Of course," she responded; her voice steady despite the fluttering in her stomach.

She had stopped using the cane a few days ago, but the limp was still ever so present and made her super self-conscious. As she walked over to him, she caught sight of Nikki, who was cradling her cat, Tabby, in her arms while talking to a gentleman she assumed was there to adopt a pet.

Just then, Nikki turned and spotted her. Her smile widened. She said something to the gentleman before taking purposeful strides in her direction.

"Hey, sunshine."

"Hey, Nikki," Trish greeted back with a warm smile. "I see you brought Tabby with you."

"Yeah. To sweeten the deal," Nikki replied, smiling down at the cat, contented with being carried around like royalty. She brought her attention back to Trish. "How are you holding up?" Her eyes held a knowing glimmer.

"I'm fine," Trish deflected, her gaze wandering back to Reed. "Just a lot going on." She felt the pressure on her arm and looked over at Nikki.

"You deserve to be happy, Trish," Nikki said, her eyes swimming with conviction. "I wish you would believe that for yourself because then you would fight for it."

Trish watched her sister walk over to the gentleman she had been talking to. What was happiness anyway?

"These are the freshly rescued pets, which means we have our work cut out for us in finding them a home,"

Reed informed her when she made it over to where he was.

Trish looked at the different breeds of dogs in the enclosure. She loved these animals. Regardless of their past hurt, neglect, and mistreatment, they all looked friendly. Their innocent eyes and unabashed affection provided a welcome respite from the complications of her life. Today, she was determined to find them each a home, a sanctuary.

"Do you think this one will find a home?" Reed asked, handing her a small, scruffy puppy. His eyes were on her face, watching for her reaction.

"I hope so," she murmured, cradling the puppy against her chest. "Everyone deserves a home, don't they?"

"Yes, they do." Reed's eyes never left her face. There was a moment of silence, a pause filled with unspoken words and emotions. The feeling of wetness on her fingers broke her out of whatever invisible force had kept their gaze on each other to see the puppy licking her fingers.

"This one definitely deserves a home today," she chuckled, handing the puppy back to Reed, who chuckled right along with her.

The day continued, the park buzzing with the chatter of potential adopters and the excited barks and meows of the animals.

"Excuse me, miss, can you tell me more about this adorable little pup?" a woman whose short black hair streaked with silver asked, her eyes sparkling with excitement as she knelt down to get a closer look at a fluffy golden retriever puppy.

With a warm smile, Trish crouched beside the woman and gently picked up the wriggling bundle of fur. "Certainly! This sweet pup is eight weeks old and full of energy. She loves belly rubs and playing fetch in the grass. She's been waiting for her forever family, and I have a feeling she'll bring a lot of joy to someone's life."

Trish couldn't help but grin as the puppy nuzzled her hand, her tail wagging furiously.

"She's absolutely adorable. I've been thinking about adopting a dog for a while, and she is the perfect fit. What's the adoption process like?" the woman asked.

Trish's eyes lit up with enthusiasm. "Oh, it's simple, really. We just have a short application form for you to fill out, and then we'll schedule a home visit to ensure it's a safe and loving environment for her. Once everything is approved, you can take her home with you."

The woman nodded. "That sounds wonderful. I'll fill out the form right away. Thank you for all the work you do here." Trish gave her a warm smile.

At the end of the day, many of the pets had been adopted, which the members of the Humane Society considered to be a success. Trish was happy for the cats and dogs that found new homes.

"Great job today, team," Reed congratulated his team. "Today was a huge success. Come tomorrow, we will start our home visits to ensure the families are ready to receive their new pets."

"Woo-hoo!" the team cheered in excitement.

"Trish," Nikki touched her elbow to get her attention. "I'm so sorry, I can't take you home."

"What? Why?" Trish asked, confusion etched on her face.

"I'm meeting Paul in the next twenty minutes. We're going to Whidbey, and I'm already running late. I would suggest you take the car from me and drive yourself ho—"

"No!" Trish rushed out, her tone frantic and eyes wide.

Nikki's lips folded in on each other as her eyes shone with sympathy. "You've got to get behind the wheel again sometime, Trish."

Trish shook her head defiantly, her eyes ignited with an unwavering determination. "Yeah, well, that won't be happening today," she declared, the strength in her words resonating through the air.

Nikki's lips parted, the anticipation of her next words hanging in the air. However, they quickly sealed together, a fleeting hesitation preventing the words from escaping. Instead, she mustered a sigh and murmured, "I kind of was expecting that." Her eyes brimmed with understanding. "Why don't I ask Reed to take you home? Reed!"

"No," Trish said at the same time Nikki called his name. "Nikki, what are you doing?" Her eyes widened, a flicker of panic dancing within them as Reed made his way over to them.

A devious smile played upon Nikki's lips; her eyes gleaming with a mischievous glint. "I'm simply ensuring you have a safe ride home," she replied, punctuating her statement with an incredulous stare, as if the answer were as plain as day.

Trish released an exasperated breath. "I didn't ask you to do that, Nikki."

"Do what?"

Her back stiffened at the sound of his voice.

"I was just telling Trish that I can't drive her home after all," Nikki replied, her lips turned up in disappointment.

"I can take her," Reed readily offered. "We just have

to round up the animals and take them back to the shelter, but after that, I am free."

"You don't have to do that," Trish stepped in, tired of them talking about her like she wasn't there.

"I want to," Reed responded almost immediately before releasing a nervous chuckle. "It's no trouble at all."

"I," Trish hesitated. The poke in her side caused her to look over at her sister, whose eyes encouraged her to say yes.

"Thank you, Reed. I appreciate it." She smiled.

"Great." He smiled back. "Let me just go help the others, and then we can go."

"I can help," she offered.

"No, no." His voice was firm but gentle, laced with a protectiveness that wrapped around her like a warm blanket. "You've been a whirlwind all day, Trish. You should rest."

Trish offered him a small smile before he walked off. She turned to Nikki. "I can't believe you ambushed me like that," she said with a scowl on her lips.

"I wasn't trying to ambush you." Her voice, though as soft as a feather, carried the weight of her intentions. "I just wanted to ensure you're in good hands." She paused, her gaze steady on Trish. "Besides, I think you and Reed need more than just fleeting greetings and events for the Humane Society to figure out where you both stand."

"Nikki," Trish groaned, a sigh of resigned exasperation escaping her lips. "I just...I can't think about that right now."

"All right...I'll leave it for now." Nikki held up her hands. "But only because I'm late for my date."

"Have fun." Trish smiled.

She watched her sister walk across the lawn before

getting into her car and driving off. She turned and made her way over to Reed. Half an hour later, he was helping her into his truck.

"The guys said they'll take the animals back, so I'm taking you straight home," he expressed as he pulled away from the park.

"Great." Her lips twitched.

"So..."

At the long pause, Trish threw him a sideways glance.

"How is the leg?"

"It's not so bad," she replied.

"I'm glad." He turned and smiled.

Trish felt her heart skip a beat, and she quickly turned her head, not wanting to dream about the possibility of something more.

"How's it going with Amy?" he asked after a long period of silence.

"Um. Things are okay between us. We still have so much to unpack as we get to know each other. But we're getting there," she replied.

"That's good to know. The last..." He looked over at her before turning his head back on the road. "The last time we spoke about her, it seemed like things were strained between you two."

"It's not great, but I think we're in a better place now," she expressed.

"That's good," he responded before the truck was shrouded in silence once more.

Trish stole a glance at Reed, their eyes meeting fleetingly, as if dancing on the precipice of unspoken confessions. She yearned to tell him how her heart skipped a beat whenever he was near, how she longed for their laughter to fill the empty spaces between their conversations. But fear clung to her like a shroud, suffocating the words that begged to be spoken.

A few minutes later, they pulled up to the house, and Reed cut the engine. "Listen, Trish, I understand you have a lot on your plate right now, and I don't want to rush you, but—"

Her heart beat wildly in her chest.

"Trish, I—"

The sound of another car pulling up cut off his sentence, and they both turned their heads at the slam of a car door to see Amy storming past the truck toward the porch, which sprang Trish into action.

"Reed, I'm sorry, but I have to go," she spoke with urgency.

"It's fine. Go. Your daughter needs you," he spoke with an encouraging smile. His gray eyes shone with disappointment, and she felt a tinge of guilt as she opened the truck door and slipped out to go after her daughter.

Chapter Ten

"Amy?" Trish called out, her voice echoing through the house. "Where are you?"

She was answered with silence, but she chose to go on the hunt for her daughter. It was clear that something had upset her. She found Amy in the kitchen with her head in the refrigerator, pulling out items.

"Amy? What's wrong?" Trish cautiously approached her daughter.

Silence greeted her once more as Amy dumped the items on the counter before heading back to the refrigerator. Then, "It's nothing," came her answer, her voice brittle and thin as dried leaves in the wind.

But Trish knew it was anything but nothing. "Amy, please," she implored, "Talk to me."

Amy straightened up and turned to her mother with a quick, piercing look, then sighed, a sound filled with so much weariness it seemed to fill the room. "It's just... I'm having some problems at school, no big deal," she shrugged, avoiding Trish's gaze.

A flare of protectiveness ignited in Trish. "Is it the guest lecturer you told me about last week? Is he still picking on you?" she asked with deep concern.

Amy nodded. "Yeah."

"Amy, it's unfair he is picking on you for no apparent reason. If you want, I could speak to Professor Reynolds about this Gabriel fellow. His wife, Sherry, and I are friends," Trish offered.

Amy cut her off, her voice sharp with resentment. "No, I don't need you fighting my battles for me."

Trish paused, taken aback. Amy's eyes had grown hard, and her stance was defensive. "Amy, I..."

But Amy didn't let her finish. "Just stop, okay? Stop trying to fix everything. You're just feeling guilty because you weren't there for me twenty-one years ago. You don't get to just jump in and try fixing my problems to be the hero. You can't...that ship sailed years ago." Her voice broke on the last sentence. Her words, harsh and bitter, hung heavy between them.

"Amy, I..."

Trish could only watch as Amy retreated until the sound of a door slamming shut with a decisive bang.

Trish stood there, her heart thumping painfully against her rib cage. She was tired, bone-deep tired. Exhausted from the Adopt-a-Pet day she had volunteered at, worn thin from the tension between her and Reed because of the unspoken feelings they both harbored—and now this—this seeming failure with Amy. It was all too much.

She turned to look at the items lying on the counter, realizing Amy had taken out ingredients typically used in baking. She decided to replace them as it was evident she had added to Amy's frustration, which probably translated into her not being interested in preparing anything. Deciding they both probably needed some space at this time, Trish went to her room, took a shower, and then made her way over to the Nestled Inn.

Trish's footsteps created a soft rhythm on the cobbled path as she approached the entrance of the inn. Entering the quaint reception area, she found Kaylyn organizing paperwork behind the front desk.

"Kaylyn," Trish greeted.

"Oh, hi, Trish. I didn't know you were back already," Kaylyn returned with a bright smile synonymous with her bubbly personality as she walked from behind the reception desk.

"Yeah. I came home a little under an hour ago."

"Okay. How was the event today? Did you guys find those adorable little pets new homes?"

"Yes. The turnout was actually better than we anticipated. Many of the pets got adopted." Trish smiled.

"That's wonderful news."

Trish nodded in agreement. "How is everything going with our guests?" she asked, changing the subject.

"Everything's fine. A few of them are in town, and two couples are at the restaurant. "Laura and Kenny are by the back porch," Kaylyn rattled off. "Dorothy left about an hour ago, but everything's under control."

"Sounds great," Trish responded, her lips turning up in a half-smile.

"Uh-oh. I know that look," Kaylyn observed.

Trish squinted her eyes in question. "What look?"

"I've had a bad experience, but I don't want to talk about it because I don't want to be a burden look," Kayly instantly replied.

Trish released a soft sigh.

"Come, sit down," Kaylyn said, gesturing to the plush armchairs arranged near the window.

Trish settled into the chair, the soft cushion enveloping her weary body. Kaylyn poured her a glass of wine before pouring one for herself.

"What's on your mind?"

She sipped her wine, savoring the crispness on her tongue before finding the courage to speak. "It's about Amy," she began, her voice tinged with sadness. "She doesn't want my help, Kaylyn. She resents me so much for not being there for her that everything I do or say seems to be a trigger for her."

Kaylyn's eyes softened with understanding. "It's a lot for her to process, Trish," she replied, gentle and empathetic. "Discovering she was adopted can be a whirlwind of emotions. Give her time to heal, dear. Be patient with her."

Trish sighed; her heart heavy with the weight of the situation. "But it's been three months, Kaylyn," she said, her voice tinged with frustration. "Shouldn't we be able to move forward by now?"

Kaylyn leaned forward, her voice reassuring. "Every person's journey is different, my dear. Amy is fragile, and her wounds are still fresh. Healing takes time, especially when it comes to matters of identity and family. Trust that she will come around when she's ready."

Trish released a heavy breath but chose not to say anything. She knew, however, what Kaylyn said was right. She had to give Amy time to come around. Only it felt like she was fighting a losing battle.

"So, what's the status on you and Reed?" Kaylyn asked, breaking her out of her thoughts.

"What do you mean?" Trish asked, eyes squinted.

Kaylyn gave her a deadpan look. "Trish, I've seen the way you and Reed tiptoe around your feelings for each other for years," she began, her voice filled with compassion. "Ever since your accident, I've watched as he's stood by your side, unwavering in his care and affection. I was certain he would've confessed his feelings for you by now."

A pained smile tugged at the corners of Trish's lips as she lowered her gaze. The memories of that fateful day echoed in her mind, the screeching tires and the shattering glass forever etched in her memory.

"He tried to..." she spoke softly, her voice laced with longing and regret. "But I... I stopped him from confessing, Kaylyn. My life has become a tangled mess of confusion, and I didn't want to burden him with it."

Kaylyn's eyes widened in disbelief, her brows furrowing with concern. "Trish, that's a load of crap!" she exclaimed, her voice filled with conviction. "You've been through so much, and Reed has been there every step of the way. Don't you think he deserves a chance to express his feelings? To be there for you?"

Trish fidgeted, wringing her hands in her lap, her heart torn between fear and longing. She closed her eyes. "I know, Kaylyn," she murmured, her voice tinged with vulnerability. "But everything feels so uncertain right now. I don't want to complicate things further. What if I can't give him what he deserves?"

Kaylyn placed a comforting hand on Trish's shoulder, her eyes brimming with understanding. "Trish, life is never certain," she said gently. "But you can't let fear hold you back from what could be your greatest happiness.

Reed cares about you deeply, and he has shown it time and again. You owe it to yourself to follow what's in your heart, no matter how confusing it may seem."

A tear escaped Trish's eye, glistening like a diamond in the fading light. She took a deep breath, feeling the weight of uncertainty burden her shoulders. "I know you're right, Kaylyn, but I don't know if I can trust my heart at the moment," Trish whispered."

Kaylyn placed a comforting hand on her arm as they sat in silence for a while.

As the sun dipped below the horizon, casting vibrant hues of pink and orange across the sky, Trish made her way back to the main house.

She could hear voices coming from the kitchen the moment she stepped into the hall.

Curiosity piqued, Trish slowed her pace and followed the voices. She spotted Amy and Nikki sitting opposite of each other in the armchairs, their silhouettes etched against the fading light from outside. Trish hesitated momentarily, her heart pounding in her chest, before deciding to eavesdrop.

Amy's voice carried to her ear, filled with a mix of frustration and vulnerability. "I just don't get it, Aunt Nikki. How could she have let them take me away? How could she have given me up?"

Nikki's reply was gentle, tinged with empathy. "Amy, you know your mom loves you. Sometimes, life puts us in impossible situations, and we make choices we never thought we would."

Amy's voice cracked; the strain evident in her words. "But it's like she's trying too hard to make up for it now. I feel suffocated, like she's constantly prying into my life, wanting to know everything. Can't she see I need space to figure things out on my own?"

Trish's heart sank, her steps faltering as the weight of Amy's words settled upon her. And there it was—her daughter resented her.

With a heavy sigh, Trish retreated silently, her footsteps barely audible against the veranda floor. She made her way to the sanctuary of her room, the walls offering solace. She understood the profound impact her decision had on Amy's life and the scars it had left behind. And while she longed for a closer bond, she realized forcing the issue would only widen the chasm that separated them.

The night settled around Trish, the darkness mirroring her somber mood.

As she lay on her bed, staring at the ceiling, Trish whispered into the silence, "I'm here, Amy. Always. Whenever you're ready, I'll be here." With that quiet promise, she closed her eyes, hoping that time would bring the healing they both desperately sought.

Just as she was drifting into a fitful sleep, a soft knock on her bedroom door startled her. Trish groaned inwardly, hoping for a moment of peace, but she knew it was Nikki. Sighing heavily, she mustered the energy to call out, "Come in."

The door creaked open, revealing Nikki's silhouette in the doorway. Trish's irritation flared up instantly, and her voice held a sharp edge as she snapped, "What do you want, Nikki?"

Nikki, seemingly undeterred by her tone, stepped into the room and closed the door behind her. "I just wanted to talk, Trish," she said, her voice tinged with concern.

"Well, I don't want to talk to you," Trish refused.

"You seem upset," Nikki observed.

"Upset? Upset doesn't even begin to cover it," Trish interrupted, her frustration boiling over. "I'm trying to build a relationship with my own daughter, and you're always getting in the way, playing the fun aunt, stealing all the attention!"

Nikki's eyes widened, hurt flashing across her face. "That's not fair, Trish," she retorted defensively. "Amy loves spending time with me, and I enjoy being a part of her life. It doesn't mean I'm trying to replace you."

"Oh, please!" Trish scoffed, sitting up in bed. "You've always wanted Amy to be your daughter. I can see it in your eyes every time you're with her. And now you're making sure she sees you as that, while I become an outsider in my own daughter's life."

Nikki's jaw tightened, and her voice turned icy. "You know what, Trish? If you hadn't given Amy up for adoption in the first place, none of this would have happened. I offered to take her, to be her mother when you couldn't handle it. But no, you chose some strangers over your own flesh and blood."

Trish recoiled as if struck. Nikki's words cut deep, reopening old wounds that she had spent years trying to heal. Tears welled up in her eyes, a mixture of anger and sadness. "How dare you throw that in my face," she whispered, her voice trembling. "You have no idea what it was like for me to make that decision. And now you're using it against me?"

Nikki's anger softened, replaced by a mix of regret and remorse. She took a step closer to Trish, her voice filled with sorrow. "I'm sorry, Trish. I didn't mean to hurt you like that."

"Can you just leave, please?" Trish interrupted her.

Nikki's lips parted as if she were about to say something, but instead, she clamped shut, and she turned and exited the room.

At the sound of the click of her bedroom door, Trish broke down in tears.

Chapter Eleven

"Good evening. Welcome to Lot 28. My name is Amy, and I'll be your server tonight. May I start you off with a glass of champagne to celebrate this special occasion?" Amy greeted the couple she had been informed was celebrating their anniversary with a bright smile, her voice warm and inviting.

The couple exchanged a glance, then nodded with enthusiasm. "That sounds delightful, Amy. We'll take your recommendation."

Amy nodded, her smile widening. "Excellent choice. I'll bring that right away. Please take your time to peruse the menu, and don't hesitate to let me know if you have any questions." With that, she left to pick up a bottle of cabernet franc.

Working at Lot 28 was a significant upgrade from the bustling diner she used to work at back in Seattle. The renowned one-star Michelin restaurant emanated an air of elegance and sophistication that never failed to amaze her. Soft lighting bathed the room in a warm glow, casting elongated shadows that danced upon the walls adorned with swirling patterns reminiscent of black-and-gold lace trimmings. The ambiance was inviting yet undeniably refined.

The tables, draped in off-white linen, were meticulously set with pristine cutlery, sparkling in the dim light. The waitstaff, like Amy, was dressed in the classic combination of black-and-white. The women wore a delicate gold collar necklace necktie, adding a touch of glamour, while the men sported a sophisticated gold cravat. The uniform not only exuded elegance but also made them feel like a cohesive team.

Paul had allowed her to venture into the kitchen, allowing her to observe and learn from his talented chefs. It gave her the chance to perfect her craft and elevate her culinary skills to new heights.

After the week she'd had, from the constant criticism from Gabriel and her standoff with her mother, she found solace in the sanctuary of Lot 28. As she gracefully moved between the tables, a sense of purpose enveloped her, and the doubts plaguing her mind began dissipating.

"Here you go. A bottle of our finest," Amy announced as she approached the couple's table once more. She turned the label so they could read it.

"This is perfect." The gentleman nodded as a smile of approval graced his lips.

That was permission enough for her to pour the wine before standing back and waiting for them to have their taste.

"This is divine," the woman purred with satisfaction.

"Thank you, Amy."

"You're both welcome." She smiled. "Would you like to order now?"

"Tell you what, since you've been so spot-on since we

arrived here, why don't you help us? What on the menu would go well with this wine?" the gentleman requested.

"It would be my pleasure," Amy replied, then offered her suggestions, describing the tantalizing flavors and expertly crafted dishes created by the talented kitchen team. Their enthusiasm mirrored her own, fueling a sense of pride within her.

As the evening unfolded, Amy engaged in lively conversations with the guests, sharing stories of the culinary wonders that awaited them. Their words of appreciation and delight filled her heart with a warmth that outshone any lingering self-doubt.

"Amy, the guest for the table reserved in the back has arrived. I need you to serve him," the maître d informed her.

"Okay, Joe. I'm on it," she replied, turning to make her way to the private section of the restaurant.

Her steps faltered when her eyes caught sight of who was there. It was Gabriel, seated by the table near the window. Her heart rate quickened within her chest, and a wave of panic washed over her. Why was he here in the very restaurant where she worked? Why was life punishing her so much? Taking a deep breath, she plastered a smile on her face as she approached his table.

"Good evening, sir. Welcome to Lot 28," Amy greeted, trying her best to maintain her composure.

Gabriel looked up from the menu, and his emerald eyes widened in surprise. "Amy? I didn't know you worked here."

Amy's smile faltered for a moment, but she quickly recovered. "Yes, I do. Can I take your order?"

Gabriel leaned back in his chair, a hint of superiority in his voice. "Perhaps this is why you're struggling in class. Your time would be better spent focusing on your studies rather than serving tables."

Amy's eyes narrowed, but she maintained her polite tone. "I appreciate your concern, Gabriel, but I assure you, my dedication to culinary school remains unwavering. Working here allows me to gain practical experience and learn valuable skills that complement my studies."

Gabriel chuckled dismissively, his arrogance practically radiating from him. "Practical experience is one thing, Amy, but don't you think it might be better to focus solely on honing your skills in the classroom? After all, you wouldn't want to jeopardize your future by spreading yourself too thin."

Amy felt a surge of frustration rise within her. She clenched her fists, desperately wanting to defend herself. She tried to control the embers of anger inside, but his critical gaze fanned them into flames, and she snapped. "My job here has nothing to do with your relentless criticism, Gabriel. My culinary skills are just as good as any other student, and you know it."

Without waiting for a response, she turned on her heel and walked away, leaving Gabriel momentarily stunned.

However, as Amy walked away, a sense of regret washed over her. She realized she had let her anger get the best of her and had been rude to a customer. She took a deep breath, mustered her courage, and decided to make amends. After all, customer service was a crucial part of her job.

As she approached the table, she noticed Paul standing nearby, engaged in conversation with Gabriel. Panic surged through her veins, and she silently prayed Gabriel hadn't revealed her lousy behavior to Paul.

Paul caught sight of Amy and beckoned her over. Nervously, she approached, her eyes darting between Gabriel and her boss. "Paul, Gabriel," she greeted them, her voice laced with unease.

Paul smiled warmly at her. "Amy, I was just telling Gabriel what a great addition you have been to Lot 28, and he told me he's the guest lecturer for your pastry class."

Amy nodded slowly, a tight smile on her lips as she waited for the other shoe to drop. Her eyes found Gabriel, who was already staring back at her, his expression unreadable.

"And Gabriel here has nothing but high praises for you. It seems you've made quite an impression," Paul interrupted their stare-off.

Amy's eyes widened in disbelief, her anxiety melting away. "Really?" she stammered, her voice barely above a whisper as her eyes darted between the two men.

Gabriel nodded a gentle smile she had never seen before transforming his face. "That's right, Amy. I've seen your talent and dedication firsthand. I might have been a tad too hard on you earlier, but it's because I believe in you. You're a very good pastry chef, and I see the potential for greatness within you."

A flush of gratitude and relief flooded Amy, replacing her earlier self-doubt. She straightened her posture, newfound confidence radiating from her. "Thank you, Gabriel," she said, her voice steady. "I appreciate your faith in me."

He nodded in acknowledgment.

Amy's eyes widened in surprise as she pointed from Paul to Gabriel. "Wait. How do you two know each other?" she asked, her voice laced with curiosity.

Gabriel took a step forward, his gaze meeting Amy's. "Paul was my mentor a few years back," he revealed, a hint of nostalgia in his voice.

"He was? You were?" Amy turned her gaze to Paul, her eyes filled with astonishment. The pieces of the puzzle were starting to come together in her mind.

"That I was," Paul replied with a chuckle. "This one here was a loose cannon, but I saw his potential all those years ago, and I couldn't be prouder of him for realizing his talent and putting it to use," he said, his voice filled with pride as he looked at Gabriel.

A rosy hue crept onto Gabriel's cheeks, contrasting with his usual composed demeanor. Amy couldn't help but marvel at the ease with which he interacted with Paul, a mix of respect and fondness visible in his eyes.

"Anyway, Gabriel, it was great catching up with you, and I'm sure we'll be seeing more of you," Paul said, his words carrying a note of certainty.

"You sure will," Gabriel replied, a note of determination in his voice. The brief exchange with Paul seemed to ignite a spark of inspiration within him.

Paul left them alone then, and Amy turned to him, not sure how to begin, as everything she'd thought about Gabriel had just been debunked by the short interaction a moment ago.

"Gabriel, I'm really sorry about earlier. I wasn't myself, and I shouldn't have treated you that way. It was completely unprofessional, and I hope you can forgive me."

Gabriel looked at her with a gentle smile, his eyes filled with understanding. "Amy, it's all right. I understand. We all have our off moments. Besides, it wasn't that big of a deal."

Relief washed over her, but confusion replaced it. "But why didn't you tell Paul about what happened? He would want to know if one of his waitresses behaved poorly."

"Despite what you may think, I don't take pleasure in making anyone feel miserable." He sighed and continued, "I understand my comments have been harsh, and I didn't mean to undermine your abilities. I've seen your dedication and passion in class, and I must admit, you have a lot of talent. I thought in my approach that I was pushing you to be better—the best. I didn't take into account that my actions were hurting you, so I understand your reaction earlier was because I triggered it, and I am sorry."

Amy's eyes widened in surprise. She hadn't expected such a response from him. "Thank you, Gabriel. I appreciate it. Now, let me take your order, and I'll make sure you have an exceptional dining experience."

Gabriel placed his order, and as Amy jotted it down, she couldn't help but feel a renewed sense of purpose. Her earlier blunder had been forgiven, and now she had the opportunity to prove herself. With determination in her eyes, she left the table to get Gabriel's order, her steps lighter than before.

As her shift continued, Gabriel remained at the restaurant, patiently waiting until the end. When Amy finally had a moment to breathe, he approached her with a warm smile. "Amy, can I offer you some advice? I've seen many talented chefs come and go, and I've learned a thing or two along the way."

Intrigued, Amy nodded, eager to absorb any wisdom he had to share. "Of course, Gabriel. I'm all ears."

Over the next hour, Gabriel imparted invaluable knowledge and insights, discussing everything from flavor profiles to plating techniques. Amy soaked it all in, her passion for the culinary arts reignited by Gabriel's guidance. It was a turning point in their relationship as mentorship and mutual respect began to take root.

"Keep pushing yourself, Amy," he said, his eyes filled with encouragement. "Never settle for mediocrity. You have the potential to be an exceptional pastry chef. Believe in yourself and never stop learning," Gabriel imparted as he shrugged on his coat and left the restaurant.

As the night came to a close, Amy couldn't help but feel grateful for the chance encounter with Gabriel. He had not only forgiven her earlier mistakes but had also seen her potential and was willing to invest in her growth. With newfound determination and a mentor by her side, Amy was ready to push herself further, striving to become the exceptional pastry chef she knew she could be.

Chapter Twelve

Trish stood on the porch leaning over the balcony, her eyes tracing the patterns of fallen autumn leaves as they danced in the crisp morning air. The vibrant hues of orange, red, and yellow were a stark contrast to the bleak mood that had settled over her. Still, she found the sight soothing, a distraction from the tension lingering from her confrontation with Nikki the other night.

At the sound of the door and footsteps echoing on the porch's floorboards, she looked over her shoulder to see Nikki approaching her with a cautious stare. Trish's heart tightened. Straightening up, she turned to her sister.

"Nikki," Trish murmured, her voice laced with a mix of sadness and caution.

Nikki stopped a few feet away, her eyes brimming with sincerity. "Hey," she spoke softly.

The corners of Trish's lips twitched, caught in an indecisive dance between a hesitant rise and a subtle downturn.

"Nikki, I—"

"Listen, Trish, I'm—"

"You go first," Trish offered. Nikki gave her an appreciative smile.

"Trish, I'm sorry," she said, her voice soft yet resolute. "I was wrong to say those hurtful things about you giving up Amy." She paused and drew in a breath before going on. "I was jealous, Trish," Nikki continued, her voice trembling with vulnerability. "I couldn't understand why you made that choice, and it ate away at me. But I see now that it was never about me. It was about you doing what you thought was best for Amy, and I shouldn't blame you for doing it."

"Thank you, Nikki. Your apology means a lot to me." Trish smiled, her heart swelling with a mixture of relief and gratitude for this moment of understanding between them. She took a deep breath, her voice steady as she said, "I am sorry too. I should not have accused you of trying to take Amy from me. I know, like me, you're just happy we got her back." Trish's voice cracked at the end as a tear slipped down her cheek.

"Hey. Hey, don't cry," Nikki implored, walking over to her and throwing her arms around her shoulders.

Trish clung to her sister like her life depended on it as the dam broke. "I wish I had been strong enough back then to say no to Dad. If I'd had a backbone, Amy wouldn't have grown up in a home where there was obviously abuse that has scarred her. I would have made sure she was loved and cared for, no matter what I had to do."

"We were all victims of his control and manipulation. You can't blame yourself for that. He should have loved us enough to protect us...but he didn't," Nikki reasoned.

The two separated, and Trish gave her a grateful smile.

"Nikki," Trish began, her voice tinged with a mixture of resignation and vulnerability, "I can't help but wonder how much our parents' influence still lingers in our lives, even after all these years since they've been gone."

Nikki nodded understandingly, her eyes reflecting the remnants of a childhood marred by deceit. "Yeah, it's hard to shake off the damage they caused. Dad, especially...he was such a terrible pretender. All he cared about was keeping up appearances in our darn social circle."

Their father, a prominent figure in the community, had mastered the art of deception, concealing his true nature behind a facade of perfection. But behind closed doors, he reveled in pitting his own daughters against each other, a twisted game designed to feed his own ego, and their mother stood by and did nothing.

"I think maybe part of me was also jealous of you," Trish confessed, looking down at her feet.

Nikki's brow furrowed; confusion etched across her face. "Jealous? Why?"

A bittersweet smile tugged at the corners of Trish's mouth as she raised her head to look back at Nikki. "Because you were always the brave one, Nikki. You went against our parents, against everything they stood for, to marry and leave the paper Dad worked for. You built your own success from scratch. I admired you, but I was also jealous. I thought you didn't see me as I wanted you to."

Nikki's eyes softened. "Trish, all those years, I never stopped loving you. I never stopped wanting to be closer to you. But I couldn't break free from the clutches of our past any more than you could."

The weight of their shared past regrets hung heavy in the air.

"I'm sorry I didn't reach out sooner," Trish apologized.

"I'm sorry too," Nikki replied with a smile. "I want to support you, Trish. I want to be the sister you deserve. Amy deserves that too."

Trish nodded, her eyes glistening with unshed tears. "I appreciate that, Nikki. I truly do."

Nikki's gaze softened, and she reached out to place a hand on Trish's shoulder, a gesture of comfort. "You should talk to Amy," she said gently. "Have an open and honest conversation with her about why you made the choices you did. Maybe it's time to get it all out in the open and start mending that relationship too. You have the chance to show her the love you've always had for her."

Trish swallowed the lump in her throat, her heart heavy, yet she dared to hope.

"I'm trying. I really am. But every time I look at her, I see my own failure. I see the pain I caused her, the lost years. It's hard to move past that."

Nikki squeezed Trish's shoulder; her voice filled with empathy. "You're not defined by your mistakes, Trish. You're defined by how you grow from them. I know Amy loves you, and she wants to build a relationship with you. Just be honest with her—about everything. It's not too late."

Trish leaned into Nikki's touch, finding solace in her sister's words. "You're right. I'll try harder," she promised.

"So what's the 411 on you and Reed?" Nikki asked with a knowing grin.

Trish blinked a few times, surprised by the question. With a sigh and a shake of her head, she responded,

"There is no 411 on Reed and me. We are still just friends," she replied, staring straight ahead.

Nikki, her dirty-blond curls cascading over her shoulders, turned to Trish with an empathetic look in her eyes. "Trish, I know it's understandable that you're hesitant to open up to Reed, to let him see your vulnerable side. But you need to consider giving him a chance. He might bring some much-needed happiness into your life."

Trish sighed, her fingers tracing the intricate patterns etched into the bench. "Everyone keeps telling me that. But it's not that simple. I have so much I need to put right. I have so much emotional turmoil and insecurities inside me, and I don't want to burden Reed with it."

Nikki leaned closer; her voice gentle yet firm. "Who's been telling you that, Trish? Who else knows the potential between you and Reed?"

Trish hesitated for a moment, her gaze darting away. "Kaylyn," she finally admitted, her voice barely above a whisper. "She's been urging me to let Reed in, to be honest with him about my struggles."

A small smile tugged at the corners of Nikki's lips. "Listen to Kaylyn. She's been here with you all this time. If anyone knows the depth of affection between you and Reed, it's her, and I am sure she wants what's best for you, as do I."

Trish's eyes met Nikki's, uncertainty shining in their blue depths. She released a heavy breath. "I'm just scared, Nikki. Scared if I let Reed in, he'll see the broken pieces of me and walk away."

Nikki reached out, her hand gently resting on Trish's trembling arm. "You keep saying you're too broken for him to want to be with you, but you have to give him a chance. You can't take that choice away from him. Trish, love isn't about finding someone who only loves the best parts of you. It's about finding someone who loves you unconditionally, flaws and all. Reed might surprise you. Give him a chance to show you you're worthy of love, even while you're feeling unworthy."

Trish's eyes shimmered as she absorbed Nikki's words. She finally nodded, a mix of apprehension and hope crossing her features. "You're right. I need to take a step forward and let Reed in. I can't keep denying myself the chance for happiness."

Nikki smiled encouragingly. "That's the spirit."

The two finally settled into the wicker chairs, enjoying the coolness of the morning and the beautiful contrast of the open, blue skies with the sea of colored leaves on the ground.

"So, what are you doing for Halloween?" Nikki's voice broke through the tranquil quiet that had settled around them.

"I was actually thinking of a quiet evening at home, enjoying the peaceful ambiance," Trish replied.

"Oh, come on. That's boring." Nikki made a face.

"Well, Kaylyn had suggested the idea of having a masquerade ball at the Nestled Inn," she expressed.

"That is a great idea," Nikki responded, pleased. "Why didn't you lead with that?" she went on to ask as her eyes glazed over with excitement. "We could transform the front hall and foyer into a magnificent setting for a grand soirée. Besides, don't you think the guests would love being a part of it?"

Trish's eyebrows furrowed in contemplation, her fingers gently tracing the intricate patterns on the chair. "I suppose the front hall and sitting area are spacious enough to accommodate such an event," she mused, her voice laced with uncertainty. "But, Nikki, think about the amount of work it would require to pull off a masquerade ball. And with less than a week to go, time is not on our side."

Nikki's eyes shimmered with determination; her voice confident yet persuasive. "Trish, I understand your concerns, but just imagine the exposure the inn would gain if we advertise it properly. We could collaborate with Lot 28 and Paul to provide the catering, and we can offer an unforgettable experience to our guests. It's an opportunity we shouldn't miss," she pressed.

Trish's eyes flickered with a mixture of hesitation and intrigue. She pondered Nikki's words, weighing the potential rewards against the demands of organizing such an elaborate affair. The soft rustle of leaves seemed to echo the flutter of her thoughts.

After a moment of contemplation, Trish finally relented, a smile tugging at the corners of her mouth. "You know what, Nikki? You might be onto something. Let's do it. Let's have the masquerade ball at the Nestled Inn."

"Wonderful," Nikki exclaimed, her palms connecting in satisfaction. "I can't wait to plan this. It is going to be completely epic."

"You sound like a child who just got stuck in a room of candy," Trish chuckled at her sister's antics.

"Are you kidding me? Parties like these were the main staple for me back in Arlington. However, nine times out of ten, I was only attending these shindigs to be there whenever a scandal broke out. But I do love a good party."

Trish chuckled again as she held the sides of the chair and attempted to rise from it. She finally got to her feet, but her healing leg felt numb, and without warning, she lost her balance and started toppling forward.

"Trish!" Nikki cried out with surprise and panic as Trish made contact with the floor.

"Ouch," she exclaimed as pain shot up her leg from where it connected with the floor.

"Are you okay?" Nikki rushed to her aid.

"Yeah. I'm fine. I just lost feeling in my leg because I had been sitting so long," she assured Nikki.

"You have to be careful. You're still on the mend," she encouraged.

Trish gripped the arm Nikki offered and stood to her feet. The two headed inside to prepare breakfast.

Chapter Thirteen

Nikki had left for her date with Paul hours ago, leaving Trish alone in the quiet house. As she wrote down "pumpkins" and "candy corn" on the Halloween grocery list, her leg ached with a vengeance, sending sharp jolts of discomfort through her body. She knew she was due for a physical therapy session, and after the fall she had the day before, it was imperative she went. But the thought of driving made her heart race with anxiety. The memories of screeching tires and the sickening crunch of metal haunted her relentlessly.

She sighed, her fingers gripping the pen tightly. Waiting until someone was available to take her to the physical therapy session seemed like the safest option, but the pain grew increasingly uncomfortable, as if her leg was screaming for relief.

"Enough is enough," she muttered to herself. "I can do this." With a deep breath, she slid off the stool. She hobbled over to her coatrack, grabbed her keys, and slowly made her way to the front door. Each step felt like a battle against her own doubts and insecurities. The weight of her decision pressed heavily on her shoulders, but she pushed through.

As she approached new her car, she could feel her heart pounding against her chest. She clutched the car keys tightly, her hands trembling slightly. "I can do this. I can do this," she chanted to herself, then slid gingerly into the driver's seat. She closed her eyes, taking a moment to gather her strength. She repeated the mantra in her mind she had picked up from one of those self-help programs she had been watching, "I am stronger than my fear. I can overcome this."

With a surge of determination, she opened her eyes and inserted the key into the ignition. The engine roared to life, sending a shiver down her spine. Trish's knuckles turned white as she gripped the steering wheel, her eyes fixed on the road ahead.

As she pulled out of the driveway, her anxiety escalated, twisting her stomach into knots. She focused on her breathing while keeping her eyes trained on the road. She could feel the sweat running down her back.

Sweat trickled down her forehead as she approached the bend, her hands gripping the steering wheel so tightly her knuckles turned pale. Her breaths came in short gasps, the world around her blurring into a chaotic haze. The blaring of a car horn startled her, and all she saw after that was the Ford pickup, the screech of tires, the impact—everything flooded back with terrifying clarity.

Trish's vision blurred with tears as her foot instinctively pressed harder on the brake pedal. Her car slowed down, almost to a halt, as she battled with her racing thoughts. "I can't...I can't...I can't do this," she wheezed.

Hyperventilating, she clutched her chest, desperately

attempting to regain control. In that moment of distress, her mind reached out for solace, and her trembling fingers instinctively dialed Reed's number.

"Hello, Trish?" Reed answered on the second ring.

"Reed," she managed to get through her chattering teeth.

"Trish, what's wrong?" Reed asked, his voice urgent and concerned.

"Can...Can you come...get me, please?" she whimpered.

"I'm on my way," Reed rushed out. The sound of a door slamming echoed through the receiver. The sound of an engine starting came almost immediately after.

"I need you to tell me where you are, Trish. Can you do that?"

"I'm at the foot of Camano Hill, just after the bend," she managed to direct.

"All right, I'm on my way. Just stay on the phone with me, okay?" he implored.

"Okay," she replied softly.

"Take slow, deep breaths, Trish. Inhale through your nose, and exhale through your mouth. You're going to be okay. Just focus on your breathing and my voice," he instructed.

"Okay," Trish repeated before drawing air through her nostrils that filled her chest before releasing it through her mouth. She could feel herself calming down, but just as quickly, it dissipated at the sound of a car horn before the vehicle zoomed past her.

"It's not working, Reed," Trish gasped. "I'm trying, but it feels like my chest is caving in. I'm scared," she confessed.

"You're not alone, Trish. I'm right there with you,

even though not physically yet. We'll get through this together. Do you remember our trip to the beach? The waves crashing, the warm sand beneath your feet?"

"Yes, I remember," Trish replied, remembering the salty breeze and the sound of seagulls. It had been a peaceful day, but it was because Reed had been there with her.

"That's it, Trish. Picture yourself there. Close your eyes and imagine the waves rolling in and out, the gentle rhythm. Let the panic wash away with each wave, just like it did that day."

Her breathing started to even out, and her eyes fluttered shut as she listened to his voice and followed his instructions. At the sound of a vehicle pulling up alongside hers, Trish's eyes flew open and she sighed in relief at the sight of Reed's van.

"Hey," Reed greeted softly, his eyes filled with compassion as he helped her out of the car. She wobbled, and his hands immediately circled her waist, keeping her upright.

"I'm sorry," she replied with a rueful smile.

"There's no need for that," Reed spoke with a nod. "I'm glad you called. I'll always be there when you need me, no questions asked," he assured her.

Trish gave him a grateful smile and allowed him to guide her to the van and help her into the front passenger seat.

In the silent sanctuary of the van, Reed's presence offered a measure of comfort to Trish. Their hands intertwined, his touch warm and reassuring. No words were necessary as they embarked on the journey to the physical therapist. Reed's strong, steady grip spoke volumes, conveying his unwavering support and understanding.

The passing scenery blurred as Reed navigated the familiar streets. Trish's mind still reeled from the traumatic memories, but her panic gradually subsided, soothed by the steadiness of Reed's presence. His unwavering grip on her hand provided an anchor, grounding her in the present moment.

Arriving at the physical therapist's office, Reed guided Trish out of the car with utmost care. His touch conveyed a tenderness that caused goosebumps to form on her skin and an involuntary shiver to go through her.

"Trish," Craig greeted with a warm smile when she walked into the examination room. "I was beginning to worry after you missed the last two sessions.

"I'm sorry about that, Craig. I got so busy that I fell behind on my schedule," she explained.

"It's understandable, but I am glad you are still interested in improving. I also noticed you're walking with a deeper limp. What happened?" he questioned with concern.

"I fell the other day," she answered.

"Okay. Make yourself comfortable. I'll be back in a few minutes to look at that leg," Craig instructed her before exiting the room.

Trish sat on the examination table; her eyes fixed on the physical therapist as he assessed her condition. The room had a sterile smell mixed with the faint scent of autumn leaves, and the muted light filtering through the window cast a warm glow on the white walls.

"Well, Trish," Craig began, his voice gentle. "I've examined your injuries, and I'm happy to say that everything seems to be okay. The pain you're experiencing is likely a result of the fall you took. It should subside gradually with time."

Trish exhaled a sigh of relief, her tense shoulders relaxing. "That's good to hear," she replied, a faint smile tugging at the corners of her lips. "I was worried it might be something more serious."

Craig nodded, understanding evident in his eyes. "It's always better to err on the side of caution, especially after a fall like that. However, I would recommend visiting your doctor to get some painkillers. They should help manage your discomfort while you heal."

Trish nodded, appreciating his advice. "I'll do that. Thank you for your help."

Leaving the clinic, Trish walked alongside Reed in silence. "I'm glad it's nothing serious," Reed said, breaking the silence.

Trish nodded and gave him an appreciative grin.

"But hey, since you're feeling better, how about we grab something to eat? My treat."

Trish considered his offer for a moment before nodding. "That sounds nice, actually. There's a small diner nearby that serves amazing comfort food. Let's go there."

As they entered the diner, the aroma of freshly brewed coffee and homemade pies enveloped them. The place was buzzing with activity, filled with locals relishing the comfort of hearty meals and engaging in animated conversations. Trish and Reed found a booth near the window, offering a view of the picturesque landscape outside.

A friendly waitress approached their table, her smile radiating genuine warmth. "What can I get you folks today?" she asked, her notepad ready to jot down their orders.

Reed glanced at Trish, a playful twinkle in his eyes.

"We'll have the day's special, please," he said, his voice carrying a touch of enthusiasm.

The waitress nodded and jotted down their request, leaving them to bask in the ambiance of the diner. Trish took a moment to observe the decor—a collection of vintage photographs adorning the walls, capturing the essence of the island's history and its close-knit community.

As they awaited their meal, Reed's gaze softened, and he reached across the table to hold Trish's hand. His voice was tender, filled with a blend of nervousness and honesty. "Trish, there's something I've been wanting to tell you for a long time," he began, his words laced with emotion.

Trish's heart skipped a beat, and her eyes locked on to Reed's. "What is it, Reed?" she asked, her voice barely a whisper.

Reed took a deep breath, his eyes shimmering with sincerity. "From the moment I first laid eyes on you five years ago, I've wanted to tell you how I feel about you," he spoke, his voice unwavering. "But it wasn't until the day you climbed the myrtle tree to rescue that kitten that everything solidified. Your courage, your unwavering care for others—it's what drew me to you. And your smile, Trish, it's like sunshine breaking through the clouds on a stormy day."

Trish blushed, her cheeks tinged with a rosy hue. She intertwined her fingers with Reed's, feeling a mix of joy and vulnerability wash over her. "Reed, I... I don't know what to say," she whispered, her voice filled with a gentle uncertainty.

"Ever since your accident, it hit me hard. I realized

how close I came to losing you, and it made me realize something important."

Trish looked up, her hazel eyes meeting Reed's gaze. "What is it, Reed?" she asked softly, her heart beating a little faster with anticipation.

Reed took a deep breath, summoning the courage to share his feelings. "I have feelings for you, Trish—more than just friendship. I can't shake the thought of what life would be like without you, and I don't want to. I want to be more than just a friend to you."

"Reed," she replied, her voice trembling slightly. "I care about you deeply too. You've been there for me through thick and thin, and I treasure our friendship. But like I said before, I can't be in a romantic relationship with you. I need to focus on myself, on getting to a point where a relationship isn't something to use to distract me from the things that need fixing in my life."

Reed's disappointment was evident in his eyes, but he nodded, his voice tinged with understanding. "I get it, Trish. I really do. You need to focus on healing and finding your own strength. I don't want to be a crutch for you. And like I told you before, I'll always be here for you, no matter what."

Trish reached across the table, her hand gently resting on top of Reed's. "Thank you, Reed. You mean the world to me. I just need to find my own way, and when the time is right, I hope we can explore what lies between us."

Reed managed a small smile, his grip tightening around Trish's hand. "I'll wait for you, Trish. I believe in us, and I believe in you. Take all the time you need. Our friendship is worth it."

Trish slumped in the passenger seat of Reed's van, her hands gripping the edge of the seat as they bounced along the gravel road leading to her house. It had been a long day, her body ached with exhaustion, and she just wanted to go take a nap.

Reed glanced at Trish; concern etched on his face. "You know, Trish, I think it might be a good idea for you to see a therapist," he said tentatively, breaking the silence that had settled between them.

Trish's heart skipped a beat at his words. She felt a surge of anger rise within her, her hands tightening their grip on the seat. "A therapist? Are you saying I'm crazy?" Her voice trembled with a mixture of hurt and indignation.

Reed's eyes widened. "No, that's not what I meant," he stammered. "I just thought it might help you... with your PTSD."

Trish's breath caught in her throat. The mention of her post-traumatic stress disorder sent shivers down her spine. No matter how she tried to push it away, bury it deep within her, it always found a way to resurface, to haunt her. And today, behind the wheel of her car, it had overwhelmed her, triggering a full-blown panic attack.

"PTSD?" Trish's voice cracked with emotion. "You think I'm weak, don't you? That I can't handle my own issues?"

Reed's van came to a stop in the driveway. His eyes searched hers, his voice filled with genuine concern. "Trish, I don't think you're weak. I just think you've been through so much, and maybe talking to someone could help you heal."

Trish's anger flared, her frustration bubbling over. "If I need advice on what to do, I'll ask," she snapped, her words laced with bitterness. With that, she flung open the van door and hopped out, her footsteps heavy with anger as she stormed toward her house.

"Trish. Wait," Reed called after her as she made her way up the porch.

Releasing a frustrated breath, she turned to face him. His eyes brimmed with confusion. "I'm sorry if what I said offended you," he started, scratching the back of his neck. "I didn't mean to do that. I'll get someone to bring your car up." With that, he turned and got back into his van before driving off.

Meanwhile, Trish stood on her porch, her anger slowly subsiding. Guilt began to seep into her veins, mingling with the regret that swirled within her. She knew she had lashed out at Reed, and he had meant no harm. But the thought of seeing a therapist sent shivers down her spine, conjuring memories she wished to forget.

She had been forced to see a therapist once before, back when she was a vulnerable teenager. Every secret, every fear she had shared, had been twisted and used against her by her own father. The betrayal had left her scarred; her trust shattered into a thousand pieces.

As the evening settled around her, Trish found herself caught between her past and her present.

Chapter Fourteen

The aroma of freshly baked pastries filled the air, mingling with the heavy anticipation in the bustling kitchen. Amy wiped her moist palms on her apron for the third time as she watched Gabriel tap the surface of her quiche before using the edge to cut it and scoop out a section of the creamy inside. He placed the fork in his mouth, scraping off the content.

"The crust lacks the delicate flakiness I expect from you, Amy," Gabriel said, his voice laced with a mix of disappointment and encouragement. "But your choice of fillings shows promise. Keep refining your technique, and you might just surprise us all."

"Thank you, Gabriel. I appreciate the feedback, and I will work on it," Amy responded, her eyes gleaming with determination. "I will perfect the crust."

His green eyes glimmered with satisfaction at her answer. He gave her a slight nod before moving on to another student.

"Whew. I was worried for you for a moment," Jill

spoke, wiping her brow dramatically. "I guess he's finally seeing your awesomeness."

A smile shadowed Amy's lips as she watched him comment on another student's pastry. "Yeah. I guess he is."

With newfound confidence, Amy turned to her station, focusing on perfecting her quiche. The kitchen buzzed with activity, the clinking of utensils and the sizzling of ingredients creating a rhythmic symphony as she and her classmates continued to make the adjustments to their quiches he'd instructed.

Amy meticulously measured each ingredient, her fingers dancing across the scale. The dough came together under her practiced touch, velvety and elastic. When she was finished, she placed the baking tin inside the oven and crossed her fingers.

As the timer chimed forty-five minutes later, Amy carefully removed her quiche from the oven. The golden-brown crust crumbled delicately under her touch, and the aroma of the savory filling tantalized her senses. A satisfied grin graced her lips. She was confident this one was far better than the first.

She watched as Gabriel made his rounds critiquing her classmate's second batches of quiche, anxiously waiting for him to make his way to her station.

"Jill, this is much better, but the crust is still a little too stiff, and the inside is runnier than it should be. However, good effort."

"Thank you, Chef Gabriel. I'll try to do better next time," Jill responded, her voice tinged with disappointment. Amy gave her friend a sympathetic look.

"That's the spirit," he encouraged before walking the few steps toward Amy. Her heart hammered against her chest. No one's quiche had met his standard so far, which made her start to doubt that hers would.

Gabriel did as he had done with her first creation, and like the last time, she held her breath as she waited for his judgment. As he chewed, his critical gaze softened, and a smile graced his lips.

"Amy, this is exceptional. Your crust is finally flaky and buttery, and the filling is seasoned to perfection. Well done."

A gasp escaped her lips as her eyes became saucers. "Seriously?" she asked, still in disbelief.

"Yes. Seriously," Gabriel affirmed with a chuckle. "Keep up the good work." With that, he walked away from her station, leaving Amy dumbfounded.

She caught some of her classmates looking on in disbelief, their eyes wide with surprise. Amy couldn't help but feel a surge of accomplishment, knowing all her hard work had paid off.

At the end of her practical session, as she headed for her theory class, she spotted Seline down the hall talking to her friends loud enough for anyone in the hall to hear.

"So what, she made a perfect quiche? What makes her so special? Gabriel is probably heaping on all those praises because he feels bad she keeps failing. He's just being nice." Seline's voice dripped with malice.

Amy's breath caught in her throat. The words struck a chord deep within her, igniting a fire of anger and frustration. No matter how much she poured her heart and soul into her creations, there was always someone lurking in the shadows eager to cast doubt and bring her down.

Silently seething, Amy turned on her heel and stormed away from the group, her face flushed with a mix of indignation and determination. She couldn't let their poisonous words permeate her mind. She had worked tirelessly, honing her skills and pushing herself beyond her limits. She deserved every ounce of recognition she received.

As she stormed through the corridor, her footsteps reverberating against the tiled floor, Amy nearly collided with Gabriel. Startled, she looked up, her eyes red and teary, betraying her emotional turmoil.

Gabriel's gaze softened as he registered her distress. "Amy, what's wrong?" he asked gently, concern etched deep in his voice.

Caught off guard, Amy hesitated momentarily, her anger and frustration warring within her. But the warmth and sincerity in Gabriel's eyes broke through her defenses, compelling her to share her burden.

"Some students... they believe that the only reason you've been 'soft' on me is that you're sorry for me." Amy's voice quivered with a mix of vulnerability and determination. "They think I'm not doing any better in this class, that I'm just a charity case."

Gabriel's eyes widened, a flicker of disbelief crossing his face. "Amy, don't listen to them," he said firmly, his voice laced with conviction. "They're detractors, envious of the hard work and talent you possess. You've proven yourself time and time again, and their words are nothing more than petty attempts to undermine your success."

A blush crept up Amy's cheeks, her heart fluttering at Gabriel's unwavering support. His words were a salve to her wounded spirit, reigniting the flicker of confidence within her.

"You really think so?" Amy whispered; her voice barely audible.

Gabriel nodded, a reassuring smile gracing his lips.

"Absolutely. You're incredibly talented, Amy. I've seen the passion and dedication you bring to this class. Trust your abilities, and don't let anyone else's doubts cloud your mind."

Amy's lips curled into a shy smile. "Thanks. I think I really needed to hear that."

"Anytime." He smiled, causing Amy's heart to flutter.

* * *

As the sun dipped below the horizon, casting a warm golden glow over Camano Island, Amy found herself bustling between tables at Lot 28, a cozy seaside restaurant. Her culinary classes had just ended for the day, and now she was balancing trays of delicious dishes, skillfully maneuvering through the crowded dining area.

"Excuse me," a middle-aged man called out, raising his hand to grab Amy's attention.

"Is everything okay with you?" she asked, looking from him to the woman sitting across from him, whom Amy assumed was his wife.

"We're ready to order," he responded.

"Okay, go ahead," Amy encouraged.

"Could I get the salmon with roasted vegetables, please?"

"Sure thing. And for you, ma'am?" Amy asked, looking at the woman.

"I'll have the same." She smiled.

"Coming right up." Amy smiled back. As she made her way to the kitchen, the savory aroma of the restaurant's specialties filled the air, mingling with the lively chatter of the patrons.

After delivering the order to the kitchen, Amy

returned to the dining area, her eyes searching. That's when she noticed a familiar face at one of the tables.

Curiosity piqued; Amy approached Gabriel's table with a warm smile. "Good evening, Gabriel. How are you enjoying your meal?"

Gabriel looked up from his plate, a twinkle in his deep brown eyes. "Amy! The food here is exceptional, as always."

Amy beamed with pride. "That's good to hear. Is there anything else I can assist you with?"

Leaning back in his chair, Gabriel sighed. "Actually, Amy, I have a different question for you. I've been on this island for almost three weeks now, and I haven't had any time to let loose. Is there anything fun to do around here? I would've asked Paul, but I need someone closer to my age's perspective."

Amy considered his question momentarily, a playful smile tugging at the corner of her lips. "Well, there's a bowling alley not too far from here. It's a great way to relax and have some fun."

Gabriel's eyes lit up with excitement. "Bowling? That sounds like a fantastic idea! Would you like to join me, Amy?"

Amy hesitated, her mind racing with conflicting thoughts. Gabriel was her lecturer, after all, and even though he was closer to her age, he still held a position of authority. But then again, it was just a friendly outing, right?

"I... I would love to," Amy said, a faint blush creeping across her cheeks. "Let me finish my shift, and we can head out together."

Gabriel nodded in agreement, and Amy went back to doing her job.

"Amy!"

At the sound of her name, Amy turned to see Sarah emerging from the kitchen, a smile on her lips.

Amy's own lips broadened to reveal her teeth as her eyes shone with glee.

"Hey, Sarah. How's everything going?"

"Oh, you know, I'm just trying to get through this pregnancy," she chuckled, her hand gently resting on her five-month-old baby bump.

"Buttercup is at it again, huh?" Amy chuckled along with her.

"Why do you think I'm here? I'm trying not to gain too much weight, but this one has other plans for me," Sarah replied, pointing at her tummy.

"Look at the bright side. You and Aaron won't ever be able to imagine life without little Buttercup again."

"That's true. Aaron is already wrapped around Buttercup's little fingers," Sarah replied, a soft smile on her lips. "Before I forget, you are coming to our gender reveal, right?"

Amy gave her a sheepish smile. "When is it again?"

"It's exactly one week after Halloween. Come on, Amy, I'm the one who should have pregnancy brain," Sarah chided in a playful tone.

"Sowy," Amy responded, giving her friend her best puppy eyes.

"All right. You're forgiven. But you better come," Sarah threatened, her tone once again playful.

"I'll be there, I promise." Amy held up her hand and crossed her fingers.

"Good," Sarah replied, satisfied. "I'm gonna get Buttercup's dinner and go."

"Okay. See you soon," Amy responded, giving Sarah a

hug and a kiss on the cheek. She watched as Sarah disappeared into the kitchen before heading back to her duties.

When her shift ended, Amy hurriedly changed her clothes, splashed some water on her face, then spritzed some D&G perfume Aunt Nikki had gifted her on her neck, behind her ears, and at the creases of her forearms before heading back to the dining room.

"Ready to go?" she asked when she stopped at Gabriel's table.

"Lead the way," Gabriel gestured already on his feet.

The two exited the restaurant, each getting behind the wheels of their cars. Amy pulled out of the parking lot, and Gabriel followed close behind.

She made her way to the lively bowling alley nestled in the heart of the Camano Commons Marketplace. With its neon lights illuminating the surrounding area, the alley buzzed with excitement and laughter. Clattering pins echoed through the air as they made their way inside.

As they entered, Amy couldn't help but feel a sense of nostalgia wash over her. The familiar scent of freshly polished wood mingled with the aroma of greasy snacks, creating a unique and comforting atmosphere. The colorful glow of the arcade machines beckoned them, promising a night filled with fun and friendly competition.

"Wow, it's been ages since I've been to a place like this," she exclaimed, her eyes wide with excitement.

Gabriel chuckled, a warm smile spreading across his face. "Yeah, me too. It's good to take a break from the usual routine and just let loose."

They approached the counter to rent a pair of bowling shoes, chatting animatedly while they waited. Once equipped with the necessary footwear, they strolled toward their assigned lane, the sound of their footsteps blending with the lively chatter of other patrons.

As they settled into their respective spots, Amy couldn't help but steal glances at Gabriel. There was an undeniable chemistry between them, a connection that seemed to transcend the boundaries of mere friendship. Yet, a slight awkwardness hung in the air, like an unspoken question waiting to be addressed.

"Hey, Gabriel," Amy finally mustered the courage to speak up, her voice slightly shaky. "I wanted to invite you to something..."

Curiosity sparked in Gabriel's eyes as he turned his attention toward her. "What is it, Amy?"

Taking a deep breath, Amy hesitated for a moment before continuing, her words laced with uncertainty. "My mother is hosting a Halloween masquerade ball at her inn. It's going to be a grand event, and I thought... I thought it would be nice if you could come."

A smile tugged at the corners of Gabriel's lips, and he nodded eagerly. "I'd love to come, Amy. Thank you for inviting me."

Relief flooded through her, and Amy couldn't help but feel a surge of happiness. She reached into her bag and pulled out a slip of paper, jotting down the directions to the Nestled Inn on Blue Mountain Road.

"Here," she said, handing the directions to Gabriel. "This will guide you straight to the place. Don't worry; you won't get lost."

As Gabriel accepted the paper, their hands brushed against each other, sending a jolt of electricity through Amy's body. She quickly withdrew her hand, a fleeting blush gracing her cheeks.

"Go ahead, show me what you've got," Gabriel said, pointing her to the balls lined up on a rack to the side.

"Get ready to be dusted," Amy threatened, entering competitive mode. She took a deep breath, focusing on her target. With a smooth swing, she released the ball and it glided down the lane, knocking down eight pins.

"Woo hoo," Amy celebrated with a jig. "In your face." She smirked at Gabriel.

"Nicely done, Amy! It looks like we're off to a good start," he spoke.

They continued bowling, alternating turns, their laughter filling the air. When it was time to go, she bid Gabriel good night and made her way home.

As she walked up the paved walkway toward the house, her eyes scanned the dimly lit porch, and that's when she saw her—Trish, sitting on the porch steps, bathed in the ethereal glow of the moonlight.

Chapter Fifteen

Amy's footsteps faltered as she approached, the weight of their last confrontation still between them. She took a deep breath, preparing herself for whatever might unfold. "Hey, Mom," she said, her voice tentative.

Trish glanced up, her eyes reflecting a mix of weariness and longing. "Hey, Amy," she replied, her voice soft. "It's a beautiful night, isn't it?"

Amy nodded, trying to ignore the awkward silence that hung in the air. "Yeah, it is," she said, taking a seat beside her mother. "Mom, are you okay?"

Trish offered a smile, but it didn't reach her eyes. "Of course, I'm fine," she said, her voice laced with a hint of weariness. "Why wouldn't I be?"

Amy sighed, frustration mingling with concern. "Mom, I can tell something's bothering you," she said gently. "We both know it's not just about what happened the other day."

Trish's smile faltered for a moment before she quickly recovered. "Really, Amy, it's nothing," she insisted, her voice wavering slightly. "Just some old memories resurfacing, that's all."

Amy's brows furrowed; her curiosity piqued. "Memories? What kind of memories?"

Trish hesitated; her gaze fixed on the moon above. "Memories of the past," she murmured, her voice barely audible. "Regrets, mistakes... things I can't change."

Amy's heart sank. She reached out, her hand hovering over Trish's arm. "Mom, I'm sorry for what I said to you about you not being able to fix what you did twenty-one years ago. I didn't mean to hurt you," she said, her voice filled with remorse.

Trish turned to face her, her eyes filled with a mix of sadness and guilt. "Amy, you don't have to apologize," she said, her voice barely above a whisper. "It's all my fault. It's my fault you even have a reason to feel this way, and I can never undo that."

Amy shook her head, frustration and sadness intertwining within her. "No, Mom, that wouldn't be fair," she said firmly.

For a moment, they sat in silence. Amy drew in a breath and released it before she spoke again. "When I found out I was adopted from Aunt Nikki, I didn't want to believe it, but then I was so angry, wondering what could have caused you to give me up. Then I learned you were in a coma, so I didn't get the chance to ask you these questions, and I had to depend on Aunt Nikki to fill in the gaps for me. Then you got better, and I just didn't know if it was worth dredging up the past while you were so fragile. So, I decided to give the questions a rest. Then, the more you tried to be there for me, the more questions I had and the angrier I became toward you. What I have learned, though, is I can't blame you for how I feel." She turned to look at her mother just then.

A flicker of pain flashed across Trish's face, and for a moment, Amy thought she saw tears glistening in her eyes. But just as quickly as it had begun to disappear, Trish's wall went back up. "Maybe you're right," she said, her voice distant. "Maybe we should just leave it at that."

Amy's frustration boiled over; her words tinged with disappointment. "No, Mom, that's not what I want," she said, her voice tinged with frustration. "I want us to have a real conversation, an honest one. But if you're not willing to open up, then I don't know what else to do."

"Ugh. This is ridiculous," Amy released a frustrated breath as she rose to her feet and trod up the steps onto the porch.

"Amy," Trish's voice was strained, a plea hidden within her name.

Amy halted, turning to face her mother. She was met with a sorrowful smile that tugged at the corners of Trish's lips.

"I'm sorry," Trish's apology hung in the air, soft as a whisper.

"Yeah. Me too," Amy echoed, her response heavy with unspoken words. With a final glance over her shoulder, she turned and disappeared into the welcoming embrace of the house.

After taking a shower, she lay in bed wide awake. As tired as she was, she couldn't sleep after her interaction with Trish. Amy wondered if she should have demanded that Trish answer her questions. It had been four months now since she found out about the adoption, and still, all she knew about why Trish gave her up for adoption was her parents made her do it. The only thing she knew about her biological father was his name. Now, here she was, living with her mother, yet she wasn't any closer to understanding the full motive behind Trish's reason for giving her up. But it was clear there was more going on with Trish. She'd looked so defeated sitting there on the porch steps with sadness dancing in her eyes.

The chime of her cell phone jolted Amy out of her thoughts. She reached for it, her heart pounding with anticipation as she saw Gabriel's name on the screen.

"Hi, Amy," the message read, **"I had a great time tonight. We should definitely do it again."**

Amy's face flushed with warmth, a mixture of excitement and nerves. She couldn't deny the surge of joy that swept through her as she read the message. It felt like a confirmation of the undeniable chemistry they had experienced during their evening at the bowling alley.

As her mind raced, replaying the shared moments, she typed her response carefully. She wanted to convey her genuine enthusiasm without coming across as too eager.

"Hi, Gabriel. I had an awesome time too, and yes, we should definitely do this more often." She winced as she sent it. **"I can't wait to see you at the masquerade…"** Shaking her head, she deleted it.

Another message came in just then.

"I'm looking forward to the masquerade and seeing you."

Her heart melted. It was official; she was falling for him—hard. Without warning, the small device vibrated in her hand as her ringtone rang out. Her heart slammed against her chest when she saw the number. She knew that number. Her thumb hesitated over the answer button as memories flooded her mind, threatening to suffocate her. Gathering her courage, she pressed answer and brought the phone to her ear.

"Hello?"

"Amy? It's me...your mother."

Her throat tightened as a lump formed, blocking the air. Clearing her throat, she tried to steady her voice as she replied, "I know it's you, Mom...how did you get my number?"

"I got it from your roommate, Sheryl," Linda answered. "Although, she did tell me you moved out a couple of months ago."

Amy ignored the question in her statement to ask, "It's been four years, Mom. Why are you calling me now?"

She could hear Linda's sharp intake of breath followed by silence. Finally, the woman replied. "Your father and I... we're getting a divorce," she spoke solemnly.

Amy's eyes widened in surprise. That was one word she never thought she'd hear from these two. No matter how badly Bob treated Linda, she always took him back. It was like she had no sense of self-preservation. Amy had hated that about her.

"Really? Wow...I'm sorry, Mom. But I'm glad you're finally putting yourself first," she spoke, her voice a mix of emotions.

There was another long pause before Linda answered. "Bob filed for the divorce, not me," she spat out, each syllable laced with bitterness.

Amy listened intently, her heart pounding in her chest.

Linda continued; her words laced with bitterness. "We were perfectly fine until I decided I wanted a baby. We were fine without a child, he said, but I wouldn't listen."

Amy's chest tightened as she waited with bated breath for her revelation.

"Then we had you, Amy, and everything changed. Bob wasn't the same. Sure, he tried to be a loving father, a responsible one. But then he just stopped trying, and I knew then...I knew he resented me for wanting you. And you didn't make it any easier challenging everything he did, painting him as the bad guy."

Amy's breath caught in her throat, a mix of shock and disbelief clouding her mind. How could her existence be the cause of her parents' crumbling relationship? She had always felt like a burden, but to hear her mother blame her directly was a blow she hadn't expected.

A wave of anger surged through her, and she couldn't hold back her retort. "So, it's my fault? Is that what you're saying, Mom? I destroyed our family by being born?"

At her lack of response, Amy had her answer. Angry tears slipped down her cheeks at the blow of not being wanted by her birth parents and the revelation her adoptive parents regretted having her. She felt broken.

"Why, Mom?" she asked, her voice trembling. "Why didn't you just tell me the truth?"

Linda's silence was a heavy pause, a moment of confusion that hung between them. "What truth?" she asked, her tone suspicious.

"That I'm adopted," Amy replied, her voice barely

above a whisper, but it resonated like a thunderclap in the silence.

"What? Who told you that?" Linda's surprise was genuine, her voice a higher pitch than usual.

"I found out a few months ago," she confessed, her voice barely above a whisper and gripped by sorrow. "I've always wondered why I looked so different from you and Dad." She touched her blond hair with ombre highlights and gazed at her blue eyes, so different from her parents' brown hair and brown eyes. "Now I understand why Dad resented me so much, why you grew to resent me too. It's because I was never truly yours."

"Where are you now, Amy?" Linda's voice was still shrill, but there was also a hint of worry seeping into her tone.

Amy let out a sigh, the tension in her body slowly easing. "I'm with my biological mother," she said, her voice steady.

"Your—your... biological mother?" Linda sputtered in disbelief, "You're with that woman who didn't want you to begin with? After everything your father and I have done for you, you choose her? How are you still so ungrateful, Amy?"

Amy felt a surge of anger, a hot wave of resentment that washed over her. "What matters, Mom, is she wants me now," she said, her voice firm and resolute. "That's more than I can say about you and Dad, the people who pretended to be my parents for twenty-one years when, in reality, you didn't even want me in the first place," she spat out.

"That's not fair, Amy, and you know it," Linda defended.

"Was it fair that you threw me out of the house after

Dad beat you to a bloody pulp when I was only trying to defend you?" she griped.

"You called the cops on your father, Amy," Linda countered.

"To Stop Him From Killing You!" At this point, Amy was breathing heavily as her tears wet her pajama top. "I tried to protect you, and you threw me out of the house and told me I was dead to you," she sobbed. "I had no one, Mom, and you didn't even care. Four years...Four long years..." Her tears blurred her vision, and her body shook from the pent-up emotions she had been holding in for so long. "I wish you had told me back then that I was adopted. Maybe I would have been able to manage my expectations and minimize the hurt I felt from your betrayal."

Linda was silent—the bitter words hung in the air, a harsh reality that could not be denied.

"Bye, Mom," took all of the energy she had left. With a sigh, Amy ended the call, pressing the red button on her phone. She turned her face into her pillow and sobbed her heart out.

Chapter Sixteen

"Tomorrow night is going to be the talk of the town. I can see it now."

"See what?" Trish asked with a raised brow as she stared at her sister, who seemed lost in a world of her own.

Nikki looked at her with sparkling eyes. "It's going to be so epic that people will look forward to next year's masquerade ball."

Trish's eyes became saucers as her lips parted with shock. "Whoa. When I agreed to do this, I didn't have it in mind that it would become a yearly event."

"Why not?" Nikki asked, a look of confusion passing over her face.

Trish released a sigh. "Because it is a lot of work, Nikki," she reasoned. "The event's tomorrow, and we're still not even close to finishing setting up for it."

"That's why you have Amy and me," Nikki replied with raised brows, as if it should have been obvious.

"I don't know," Trish replied, still hesitant.

"Tell you what," Nikki said, placing her hands on

Trish's shoulders as she stared at her encouragingly. "Let's get through tomorrow, and when you see how successful it is, I'm sure you'll be singing a different tune."

"We'll see," Trish replied before asking, "Have you seen Amy this morning?"

"Yeah. She's in her room. I knocked on her door earlier, and she said she's a bit tired, so she'll be foregoing our trip into town," Nikki replied.

"Oh," Trish said simply, trying but failing to mask her disappointment.

"I take it from your expression you haven't spoken to her," Nikki surmised.

Trish released a heavy sigh. "I'm trying to, but everything has just been so...hard," Trish confessed.

"Trish—"

The sound of the doorbell interrupted their conversation.

"That must be Kaylyn," Trish said, making her way toward the front door. However, instead of her petite, rosy-cheeked, black hair streaked with gray—worn like a badge of honor—manager and friend, stood someone with a fully black head of hair and who was at least half a foot taller than Kaylyn, but with an equally radiant smile as what she would have worn.

"Hi, Ava," Trish managed to say, her voice tinged with a mix of surprise and curiosity. "What a pleasant surprise."

"Hi, Trish. I know it's unexpected that I'm here, but I wanted to surprise Nikki," Ava responded with a bright smile. "Is she here?"

"Yes. She's in the living room. I'm sure she will be very happy to see you." Trish ushered Ava inside and led her down the hall to the living room.

"Hi," Ava greeted Nikki, who was seated on the couch, a notepad on her lap, a pen in her hand, and her head down.

Nikki's head snapped up almost immediately, eyes wide with surprise. "Ava? What are you doing here?" she asked, rushing over to the woman and pulling her into a tight hug.

"What do you think? I couldn't miss this party you've been raving about," Ava spoke as they separated. "I haven't even attended a social event since you left Arlington. It doesn't feel the same," she pouted.

"You know you could always move here to the Island. That way, we could carry on with our shenanigans," Nikki spoke with a suggestive grin.

"I would take you up on that offer if there weren't so much going on in my life back home."

"I know," Nikki nodded with understanding. "In any case, I'm happy you're here because it's now guaranteed we're gonna have an amazing time tomorrow."

Trish stood by the doorway watching their interaction and couldn't help but feel left out. Her sister had a life that hadn't included her for many years, and Ava had been in her life for more than ten years now. Yet as Nikki stood there with her best friend, their bond palpable, Trish couldn't escape the yearning that consumed her. She felt like an outsider, a mere spectator to their easy connection, while they effortlessly portrayed the sisterly bond that should have been hers.

"So, what's the plan for today?"

Ava's question pulled Trish out of her dark thoughts.

"We're headed into town to pick up some more decorations and get our dresses and masks," Nikki answered.

"Sounds like fun. Mind if I tag along?" Ava asked.

"Not at all," Nikki responded. "Right, Trish?" She turned questioning eyes to her sister.

"Of course. You're welcome to join us, Ava," Trish replied with a welcoming smile. Ava returned her smile.

The three women exited the house and got into Nikki's car, then drove over to the Nestled Inn to pick up Kaylyn and head for town.

As soon as they drove into town, it was buzzing with excitement as people filled the streets and shops, no doubt preparing for the festivities. Trish stepped out of the vehicle, admiring the scene.

Downtown Camano was adorned with colorful fall decorations, and the aroma of spiced apple cider wafted from nearby cafés, mingling with the scent of fallen leaves. The sun cast a warm glow on the charming storefronts, each one beckoning the ladies with promises of Halloween treasures.

The storefronts were adorned with vibrant orange-and-black decorations, spiderwebs draped across windows, and spooky silhouettes of witches and ghosts. Pumpkins of all sizes and shapes were scattered throughout, their carved faces illuminated by flickering candles. The air carried the scent of freshly baked goods, a tantalizing mix of cinnamon, spices, and sweet treats.

The women approached the boutique, Mystique Couture. The bell above the door tinkled as they stepped inside, greeted by the melodious voice of the shop owner, Mrs. Hawthorne. "Welcome. Welcome. Ah, Trish, it is so good to see you," she chimed, walking up to Trish and taking her cheeks between her palms before tilting up to kiss either side of her face.

"Hi, Mrs. Hawthorne. It's good to see you too," Trish returned with a bright smile before turning to the rest of her party. "You remember my sister, Nikki." She gestured. "And this is her friend, Ava."

"Hello, dears." The woman smiled at them welcomingly. "And Kaylyn, so good to see you." Her eyes fixed on Kaylyn.

"Hi, Martha," Kaylyn responded with a slight nod.

"What can I do for you, ladies?" Her eyes averted to Trish as she asked.

"We're here to find the perfect masks and costumes for our Halloween masquerade ball at the inn tomorrow," Trish informed her.

Mrs. Hawthorne's eyes sparkled with delight. "Ah, the masquerade ball! There's been quite a buzz around town. You've come to the right place. Let me show you our latest collection."

The women followed Mrs. Hawthorne, who pointed them to some intricately designed gowns and masks that embodied the masquerade's theme of horror and elegance.

Trish, drawn to a corner of the store, spotted a magnificent mask adorned with feathers and sparkling gems. As she picked it up, she couldn't help but imagine herself as a mysterious, alluring figure hidden behind its beauty.

She carefully placed the mask over her face before heading to where the others were. "What do you think?" she asked with hopeful anticipation.

"You look like a mysterious enchantress in this," Ava exclaimed, her eyes shining with delight.

"I agree," Nikki joined in, and Kaylyn nodded in approval.

"I have the perfect dress to go with that," Mrs. Hawthorne spoke up before she went over to a rack and came back with a dress that would definitely be a show-stopper.

"Wow," was the only word that managed to escape Trish's lips.

"She's taking that dress," Nikki decided, her tone final.

An hour later, they left the boutique, each with a garment bag in hand. The women lingered on the walkway, stopping every so often to admire the displays in the storefronts. Trish walked ahead of them on a mission to get their last-minute shopping done in time.

As she turned a corner, Trish's eyes widened, and she almost stumbled upon seeing Reed standing before her. Her heart skipped a beat, and she tried to gather her thoughts.

"Hey, Reed," Trish said, her voice strained with a mix of nervousness and regret.

"Trish," he replied cautiously, his tone mirroring her own.

The air between them crackled with unspoken tension, the weight of their unresolved issues hanging heavily in the air. Trish's heart pounded in her chest, regret gnawing at her as she struggled to find the right words.

Before she could summon the courage to speak, Nikki intervened, her voice filled with friendly enthusiasm. "Reed! It's great seeing you here."

"Hi, Nikki," he greeted her with a warm smile. "I had some business to take care of," he further explained.

Nikki nodded in understanding. "Will you be attending the Halloween masquerade ball at the Nestled Inn?"

Reed's eyes momentarily shifted away from Nikki to

Trish, a flicker of disappointment crossing his face. "I don't think I'll make it," he replied, his voice tinged with regret. "But I'll do my best to swing by if I can."

Trish's disappointment was palpable. She had secretly hoped to see Reed at the ball, to have a chance to mend the rift between them. But his uncertain response dashed her hopes.

"Ah, bummer. I was really hoping you'd be there to help us gals out, you know, with like crowd control," Nikki sighed dramatically, earning a chuckle from Reed.

"I appreciate the thought, Nikki. Maybe next time," he spoke to Nikki, but his eyes were on Trish, probing.

Trish felt her heart rate start to accelerate again, and she averted her eyes.

"It was great seeing you, Nikki, Ava, Kaylyn," she heard him say. "Trish," he finally called her name, which caused her to raise her head to look into his gray eyes. "I'll see you." His words seemed to hold promise.

"Bye, Reed," she spoke softly.

As Reed excused himself and walked away, Nikki turned to Trish, her eyes filled with concern. "Trish, what was that about? You two were acting weird around each other."

Trish's defenses went up instantly, her voice laced with defensiveness. "I don't know what you're talking about, Nikki. Reed is a busy man, that's all."

Nikki's gaze lingered on Trish for a moment, her piercing blue eyes searching for the truth. But sensing Trish's reluctance to share, she shrugged her shoulders.

"Okay," she said simply.

Trish, Nikki, Ava, and Kaylyn arrived home, their arms laden with shopping bags filled with Halloween decorations. Excitement filled the air as they made their way to the Nestled Inn.

The sun was setting, casting long shadows across the front yard, and a crisp autumn breeze rustled the colorful leaves. Carved pumpkins that would serve as lanterns lined the pathway leading to the entrance of the inn, setting an eerie yet inviting atmosphere.

The group stepped into the foyer and made their way into the spacious hall and sitting room, where a large table stood in the center, ready to be transformed into a Halloween extravaganza. They unpacked the shopping bags, revealing a kaleidoscope of decorations—black cats, glowing skeletons, and cobwebs galore.

Kaylyn unfurled a roll of purple and silver streamers, twirling them around her fingers. "Where should we put these?" she asked, her eyes scanning the room for the perfect spot.

Ava pointed to the fireplace mantel. "I think they would look fantastic draped over the mantel, don't you?"

Kaylyn nodded enthusiastically. "Great idea, Ava. Let's do it!"

They worked in silence, their movements synchronized, and the room gradually transformed into an elegant but haunted haven. Spider webs stretched across every corner, skeletal heads grinned mischievously from table-tops, and flickering candles promised to cast eerie shadows on the walls. Hours flew by, and as they put the final touches on the decorations, the room took on a mystical charm.

"Thank you, everyone," Trish said, her voice filled with warmth. "I couldn't have done this without all of you."

The others smiled and nodded in response.

"Hey, how come I haven't heard from Amy since I got here this morning?" Ava questioned,

Nikki's brows furrowed in confusion. "Come to think of it, you're right. When we left, she was in her room, but she had promised to come help us set up. I don't know what's going on with her."

Trish's heart skipped a beat as a pang of guilt washed over her. It was obvious Amy was trying to avoid her.

Ava shrugged; her voice filled with reassurance. "She's young. Maybe she just needs some time alone."

Nikki sighed, her worry evident in her voice. "I suppose. But it's just weird that she didn't even swing by the Nestled Inn to help us out. We could use an extra pair of hands."

Ava's eyes sparkled mischievously. "Maybe she's got a secret boyfriend and is off having some fun."

Nikki's face darkened, her voice laced with bitterness. "After everything that happened with Jake, I highly doubt it. She's been through too much to get involved in something like that right now."

Trish nodded in agreement when her sister's eyes landed on her. "Nikki's right. She's been through so much these past couple of months. Having a boyfriend is probably the furthest thing from her mind."

Trish, Nikki, and Ava headed for the main house while Kaylyn remained at the Nestled Inn to deal with the guests there. As they walked through the front door, their attention was drawn to the sound of ABBA's catchy tunes drifting from the living room. There sat Amy, engrossed in the movie *Mama Mia*, her eyes fixed on the screen.

Nikki grinned as she approached Amy. "Ah, there you are! We were wondering where you've been."

Amy looked up, a faint smile gracing her lips. "Sorry, guys. I needed a little escape. *Mama Mia* always does the trick."

Trish couldn't help but notice the strain in Amy's voice and the worry etched on her face.

"Hi, Ava," she greeted the moment she realized she was there.

"Hi, Amy," Ava returned.

"Is it okay if we join you?" Nikki asked.

"Sure," Amy replied, scooting over to the edge of the couch.

As the movie played on, the women settled themselves around Amy, their laughter mingling with the music. Yet, Trish couldn't shake the feeling that her own secrets and the weight of the past were weighing heavily on Amy's heart. She resolved to find a moment— a quiet moment after the ball—to sit down with Amy and explore the emotions that had been stirred by their newfound connection.

Chapter Seventeen

"Wow! Trish, you look amazing," Nikki excitedly exclaimed.

"You think so?" Trish asked, looking down at herself as the niggling self-doubt made an appearance.

"Yeah, Mom. You do. You look amazing," Amy, who stood beside Nikki, agreed. Her lips lifted into a smile.

"Thank you," Trish replied appreciatively. She carefully adjusted the delicate lacelike cobwebs that adorned her black-and-gold dress, ensuring they draped gracefully over her shoulders. The intricate patterns shimmered under the soft light in the hall, casting an eerie glow on her figure.

"You both look beautiful," she went on to compliment the two women.

Nikki wore a blood-red dress that flowed elegantly around her, with her hair piled on top of her head in a high bun and tendrils of sandy-blond curls falling at the sides. Her lips were painted a shade darker than her dress, and in her hand, she held a half-faced crimson mask adorned with intricate swirls and feathers. Beside her, Amy wore a black silk faille gown with off-the-shoulder puffed sleeves. Her hair was bone straight and fell down her back. In her hand, she held a black lace mask with an intricately designed red rose framed by feathers attached to one side.

"Thanks," Amy and Nikki responded simultaneously.

"We clean up well," Nikki added.

"Where's Ava?" Trish asked, looking around.

"Right here, my darlings," Ava announced, descending the stairs just then. Her costume was even more elaborate than the three women at the bottom of the stairs combined. She wore a Victorian Rococo ball gown, with Renaissance Medieval embroidery in red with gold on the flaps and hem of the dress, and lace fringes on the ends of the sleeves. Her mask that was already fastened to her face was ivory and gold.

"Now that is a showstopper," Nikki exclaimed.

Ava's colorful laughter filled the hall. "You all look extraordinary," she complimented them.

"We need to go, guys. I'm sure people are already arriving," Trish advised.

"Come on. Let's go," Nikki replied, turning toward the door.

The women stepped out into the cool autumn evening. The orange glow of the pumpkin lanterns lined the path leading to the inn, casting eerie shadows on the ground. Ghostly figures and skeletal decorations adorned the hedges, their ghoulish forms swaying gently in the cool breeze. The sweet scent of burning candles filled the air, intermingled with the earthy aroma of fallen leaves.

As they stepped inside the Nestled Inn, Trish's heart swelled with pride and awe at the transformation they had achieved. The once-ordinary hall and foyer had been completely metamorphosed into a realm of enchantment. The walls were draped in rich, dark fabrics adorned with twinkling fairy lights that danced along the edges. Ghostly silhouettes floated from the ceiling; their ethereal movements captured in the soft glow of candlelight.

The guests, both from the inn and the town, mingled throughout the transformed space, their masks adding an air of mystery and intrigue. Laughter and animated conversations filled the air as the attendees reveled in the festivities. Trish noticed a couple, their faces hidden behind intricate masks, twirling gracefully on the dance floor to the haunting melody of a waltz.

"I can't believe how incredible this is. It's like stepping into a different world," Amy exclaimed, unable to contain her enthusiasm.

"I agree," Ava added with a nod.

Trish spotted Kaylyn heading in her direction with a wide smile. Her dress shimmered in shades of blue, and her mask, a delicate masquerade butterfly, enhanced her beauty. "Trish, I can't believe how well the decorations turned out," she exclaimed, her voice filled with excitement. "It's like we've stepped into a magical realm!"

Nikki grinned, her eyes glinting mischievously. "I told you this party would be unforgettable."

"Come." Kaylyn gestured to Trish. "The guests are waiting for you to say a few words."

"What?" Trish's eyes widened with surprise. "I didn't know I had to prepare a speech," she panicked, already dreading the eyes that would be on her once she was front row and center.

"Trish, relax. I'm sure whatever you say will be great. You're a natural at this," Nikki encouraged her.

Trish released a heavy sigh before squaring her shoulders. "All right, I'm ready," she spoke with conviction.

With their masks securely in place, the trio ventured farther into the enchanting masquerade, ready to immerse themselves in the mysterious allure of Halloween night.

Trish made her way up the steps until she was standing along the balcony of the first floor. Eyes stared up at her from behind their masks, and a shiver ran down her spine. Pushing past her rising anxiety, she opened her mouth and spoke. "Good evening, everyone. My team and I are truly honored that you could join us in celebrating this night. Please enjoy yourselves, and if there are any complaints, you take it up with management." She received many chuckles at her last statement, raising the glass of champagne Kaylyn had slipped into her hand. "Let the fun begin," she announced, receiving loud applause from the guests. She descended the steps.

"Great speech."

"Thank you."

'Wonderful party. You did a great job."

"Thanks." Trish smiled and greeted the guests while responding to their compliments about the party.

As she twirled through the sea of masked faces, Trish's eyes locked on to a familiar figure standing near the punch bowl. It was Nelly, her parents' long-time friend, adorned in an elaborate Victorian gown with a feathered mask that concealed her eyes. Trish's heart skipped a beat, and a warm smile spread across her face as she approached Nelly.

"Nelly!" Trish exclaimed; her voice filled with joy. "I can't believe you made it! You look stunning!"

Nelly turned toward Trish, her eyes sparkling with delight. "Oh, my dear Trish! Your party is simply marvelous. You've truly outdone yourself," she said, her voice filled with genuine admiration.

Trish blushed. "Thank you, Nelly. I'm so glad you could be here. It means a lot to me."

Nelly's expression softened, and she placed a gentle hand on Trish's arm. "There's something I need to tell you, my dear. Something about your father," she said, her tone tinged with a hint of seriousness.

Caught off guard, Trish's smile faltered, and a mix of curiosity and fear flickered in her eyes. "What is it, Nelly?" she asked cautiously, her voice barely above a whisper.

Nelly hesitated for a moment, her gaze fixed on Trish's face, searching for the right words. "It's something you should know, something that might change the way you see him," she said, her voice laced with a hint of sorrow.

Trish's heart sank, her weariness seeping into her voice. "I appreciate your concern, Nelly, but I don't want to know," she said, her words laced with determination. "After all my parents have taken from me, I can't give them the power to continue doing it. They're gone, and I need to move on."

Nelly nodded; her eyes filled with understanding. "Perhaps you're right, my dear. Perhaps it's better left unsaid for now," she said gently, her voice carrying a bittersweet note as she patted Trish's arm.

Trish breathed a sigh of relief, grateful for Nelly's understanding. "Thank you, Nelly. Maybe another time when I'm ready," she whispered, her voice filled with a mix of gratitude and uncertainty.

Nelly smiled warmly; her eyes filled with a grand-motherly affection. "Of course, my dear Trish. Whenever you're ready, I'll be here," she reassured, her voice filled with unwavering support. "But tonight, let's focus on celebrating life, shall we?"

"That I can do," Trish answered with a soft chuckle.

Trish stepped away from Nelly a few minutes later, her mask concealing the myriad of emotions swirling within her. As she weaved through the crowd, her eyes caught a glimpse of Melissa. The woman's mask was a delicate lacework of iridescence, artfully concealing her face. However, her distinct laughter—a nasal sound—betrayed her identity. Melissa was the entrepreneur who owned a B&B on the opposite side of Camano Island. The very same Melissa was a formidable adversary in their small business rivalry, whose competitive spirit was as fierce as a riptide. Trish had always regarded her with a mix of admiration and indifference, choosing to focus on her own inn's success rather than engage in petty rivalries.

A pang of discomfort tightened around Trish's heart when she noticed the masked gentleman dressed like Zorro, complete with a flowing black cape and a glinting rapier at his side, Melissa was in deep conversation with. Recognition flooded her as she noticed the way he tilted his head while laughing, a signature tell of the man she had lost her heart to. She watched as Melissa, with a touch as subtle as a ripple in the water, placed her hand on Reed's arm.

There was a bitter taste in her mouth as she watched Melissa's flirtatious laughter infect Reed. It was like watching a scene from a film she hadn't auditioned for. Trish felt regret gnaw at her insides.

With a heavy heart, she slipped away from the spectacle, escaping into the cool autumn night outside. The sharp nip of the air was a welcome relief, a stark contrast to the suffocating ambiance of the masquerade.

Her mind raced with questions. Why was Reed talking to Melissa? What could they possibly have in common? And why didn't Reed let her know he would be at the party?

The moon cast an ethereal glow over the sprawling gardens as she leaned against the stone balustrade, her thoughts in turmoil.

A gentle breeze rustled through the trees, whispering secrets that only the night could hear. Trish closed her eyes, trying to steady her racing heart. She could still hear the distant laughter and music seeping out from the party. At that moment, all she felt was a sense of loss, a melancholy realization that she was alienating the people she cared for the most.

"Trish?"

The voice, tinged with concern, pulled her from her reverie. Trish turned to find Reed standing there, his Zorro mask removed, revealing his striking features and the warmth in his gray eyes.

"I saw you come out here," he said, his voice soft and filled with a hint of vulnerability. "Is everything all right?"

Trish swallowed the lump in her throat, struggling to find the right words. "I... thought you weren't coming," she responded, her voice barely above a whisper as she hugged herself.

Reed reached up to scratch the back of his neck as he released a silent breath. "To be honest, I didn't plan to. It was sort of a last-minute decision. I wanted to support you on your big night." His eyes bored into her as he spoke, filled with a vulnerability she had never seen in him before.

"I saw you with Melissa," she confessed, her voice again barely above a whisper. "I thought... You looked like you were having a lot of fun in her company."

Reed's eyes widened with surprise, a flicker of realization crossing his face. "Trish," he said earnestly, taking a step closer to her. "Melissa and I were just catching up. There's nothing more to it, I promise."

Trish felt a mix of relief and hope surge through her like a rekindling flame in the darkness. She dared to meet Reed's gaze, searching for the truth in his eyes.

"I haven't been able to look or think about another woman except for friendship for quite some time now. You wanna know why?" he asked, his gray eyes fixed on her.

As Trish opened her mouth to respond, something caught her eye.

"I'm so sorry, Reed. Can we pick this up at another time? There's something I need to do." She quickly excused herself, leaving behind a puzzled Reed under the haunting glow of the moon, the masquerade's echoes fading away behind her.

Chapter Eighteen

The Halloween masquerade ball was in full swing, with an air of mystery and excitement filling the grand hall of the inn. The flickering candlelight cast eerie shadows on the walls, and the haunting melody of a violin echoed through the room as the vibrant crowd of masqueraders laughed and chatted while some took to the dance floor, swaying to the symphony.

Amy's eyes darted from one masked face to another as she searched for Gabriel. It had been over an hour since she arrived at the Nestled Inn, and she hadn't caught one glimpse of him. She was starting to wonder if he was even there—if he had changed his mind about coming.

Then, through the crowd, she spotted him, dressed as the iconic Phantom of the Opera, standing near the refreshment table, a white half-mask covering the right side of his face. Amy couldn't help but gasp at his striking presence. His tailored suit accentuated his broad shoulders, and a crimson-lined cape cascaded down his back, adding an air of mystery to his appearance.

As if sensing her presence, Gabriel's eyes fell upon Amy. A smile tugged at the corners of his lips. He approached her with a confident stride, his voice carrying a hint of theatricality. "My lady, you are the epitome of elegance and beauty. A rose among thorns."

Blushing, Amy replied, "Thank you, kind sir. Your costume is equally captivating. The Phantom's allure suits you well."

"I know," he replied, a smirk playing on his lips.

Amy chortled then. "Are you always this sure of yourself?"

His green gaze became serious as he stared at her. "I have to be. Otherwise, I'd live my life always second-guessing myself and my choices."

Amy nodded in understanding.

"You look absolutely stunning," Gabriel complimented once more, his voice carrying a hint of admiration.

Amy blushed, feeling a warmth spread through her cheeks. "Thank you," she replied, her voice laced with a mix of shyness and excitement.

With a graceful bow, Gabriel extended his gloved hand toward her. "May I have this dance?"

Amy hesitated, her eyes flickering with a mixture of anticipation and self-doubt. "I have to warn you. I'm not much of a dancer. I tend to have two left feet."

He chuckled warmly. "Not a problem. I'm an excellent teacher. I'll have you waltzing around this room in no time," he spoke with self-assurance.

"Are you up for the challenge?" Amy smiled up at him.

"Always." Intense emerald eyes stared back at her as he held out his hand for her to take. Her breath caught in her throat as the words spoken between them just now took on a different meaning.

With a shy smile, she placed her hand in his, and they made their way to the dance floor. The haunting melody of a waltz filled the air. Gabriel took her hand in his while the other rested in the middle of her back. Amy's cheeks flushed as they drew closer, the warmth of his touch enveloping her. The scent of his cologne, a sweet yet masculine aroma that was uniquely his own, beckoned her to move closer, but she fought the urge, keeping herself aloof.

'Ready?" Gabriel asked, pulling her out of her thoughts.

Amy raised her head to look at him as she replied, "I'm not...but I trust you."

"Just follow my lead," he instructed as he gently guided her through the steps. However, Amy's prediction proved true as she unintentionally stepped on his foot, triggering a symphony of laughter from both of them. He twirled her around the space a few more times, but each time, she managed to step on his foot.

"I told you I was a klutz," she said with a pitiful look.

"We've only just started. You'll get the hang of it in no time," he encouraged her. However, that was not the case as the torture on his feet continued.

"Maybe we should try a different approach," Gabriel suggested. "How about we forget about the traditional dance job and do what's comfortable?"

Amy's eyes sparkled with amusement as she nodded. "I'm surprised we lasted this long before you conceded," she said, her voice tinged with playful sarcasm.

"Who said I conceded?" he replied, a playful twinkle in his eyes mirroring her own amusement. "I am simply switching my approach and starting you from the basics."

Amy couldn't control the snort of laughter that escaped her lips. She quickly covered her mouth, trying to contain her amusement, but it burst out again. "I'm sorry," she managed to say between snorts, her hand held out before her in an apologetic gesture.

Gabriel's lack of response caught her off guard. She lifted her gaze to meet his intense stare, her breath catching in her throat and her heart skipping a beat. Emotions swirled in his eyes, a mixture of amusement, fondness, and something else she couldn't quite decipher. Time stood still as they locked eyes, a silent understanding passing between them, their connection growing stronger with each interaction.

Suddenly, someone crashed into Amy, sending her stumbling forward and effectively severing the invisible thread that had connected them.

Gabriel took a step toward her, his eyes filled with concern, but hesitated for a bit, unsure of how to proceed.

"I'm so sorry, dear. I hope I didn't hurt you," a gentleman dressed in a tuxedo, a top hat, and a face mask covering his eyes apologized.

"It's okay. You didn't," she assured him with an upturn of her lips.

The gentleman, seemingly satisfied with her response, bowed his head with a tilt of his hat and continued dancing with his partner.

Amy turned to Gabriel, who held out his hand to her. Without a word, she fit her smaller hand into his larger one, allowing him to pull her closer once more. This time, they abandoned the rigid steps and began rocking to the music, their eyes connected once more. At that moment, time seemed to stand still as they lost themselves in each other's company.

After leaving the dance floor, Gabriel went to get Amy something to drink. He returned with a glass of punch for her.

"Thank you." She smiled.

"Wanna get out of here for a while?" he asked.

"What do you have in mind?" Amy tilted her head in curiosity.

"Just a walk outside to get some fresh air," he responded with an inviting smile.

"Okay," Amy agreed. She followed him through the crowd until they made their way out onto the back porch.

The night air was crisp, carrying with it the scent of autumn leaves. The full and luminous moon cast a silvery glow upon the lawn, guiding their steps. The farther away they got from the inn, the more distant the sound of laughter and music became until they faded into silence.

"It's so quiet now," Amy mused.

"Yeah. It is," Gabriel agreed. "It's a nice change of pace too...at least for a while," he added.

As they continued to walk, they fell into a comfortable silence. They soon came upon a garden still fresh with blooms. To the other side of it stood a small gazebo nestled among blooming flowers. Light filtered through the latticework, casting a mesmerizing pattern of light and shadow on the ground.

"Why don't we stop for a while?" Gabriel suggested.

"Sure," she replied.

Gabriel helped her up the steps before coming to stand by her. Though Amy couldn't see it, she could hear the sound of the ocean in the distance, the waves crashing against each other, but in a way, it felt peaceful. She pulled off her mask to savor the wind blowing against her face.

"This place...it's breathtakingly beautiful," Gabriel murmured as he pulled off his mask.

"It is," Amy agreed as a smile lifted her lips.

"Your mother was smart to buy this place."

Amy nodded in response. "I should introduce you two."

"I'd very much like to meet the woman who gave birth to such a beauty," he responded. Amy's cheeks warmed despite the cold.

A pause lingered between them, filled with the rustle of the trees that bordered the property and the distant call of a night owl. "I'm not sure she would be as eager to meet you though," she spoke softly, her gaze flitting toward him.

"Why not? Mothers love me," he joked, leaning casually against the gazebo column as he stared at her. Amy faced him and noticed the challenging smirk on his lips illuminated by the moon's soft glow.

She couldn't help but smile at his confidence. "Not after how I described you to her," she confessed, her smile turning apologetic.

His laughter echoed through the night, and Amy admired how his chest moved up and down and his lips parted to release the sound. It made her heart beat a little faster.

"I'm sure that once she meets me, she'll have no problem warming up to me, as you did," he spoke with a charming grin.

A blush crept up her cheeks, but Amy managed a small, "I don't doubt it."

A sudden gust of wind swept over Amy, causing her

to shiver. Without a word, Gabriel loosened the cape around his neck and draped it over her shoulders. The material was warm and comforting, saturated with his scent.

"Thank you," she smiled up at him.

"My pleasure," he replied, his voice a low timbre.

The wind playfully blew a few strands of her hair across her face. Before she could sweep them away, Gabriel's hand gently brushed them aside. His touch sent a jolt of warmth through her. His palm lingered against her cheek, and Amy leaned into him as his face came closer to hers.

"Gabriel..." Amy began. Their faces were inches apart, their breaths mingling in the crisp night air.

"Shh..." Gabriel whispered, his thumb gently brushing against her cheek. The tender gesture made her heart race even faster.

Before their lips could finally meet, a voice shattered the moment. "Amy!" Trish exclaimed, her voice filled with surprise and accusation.

Startled, Amy and Gabriel pulled away, their faces flushed with a mixture of embarrassment and frustration. Amy stepped back from Gabriel and turned to face her mother.

"Mom, what are you doing out here?" she asked.

"I saw you leave the party, so I came to check on you... to make sure you're safe." Trish's eyes shifted from her daughter to Gabriel, a shadow of wariness passing over her face as she stared longer at him.

"Hi. You must be Amy's mother. I'm Gabriel," Gabriel introduced himself with a charming smile, and his hand extended to her.

Trish squinted before her eyes widened as she turned

her gaze back to Amy, completely ignoring Gabriel's hand.

"Your lecturer?" Trish asked, her tone accusatory. "Amy, what is wrong with you?"

Amy felt her anger surface as her arms crossed over her chest. "What's that supposed to mean?"

Trish released a frustrated breath. "Isn't this the same man you said was picking on you at school and undermining your work? How are you now all of a sudden so chummy?"

"All right. I think that's my cue to give you some privacy to work this out," Gabriel gave out. "Ms..."

"Murphy," Trish supplied.

"Ms. Murphy. I feel awful about the way I treated your daughter. I do. I thought it was necessary at the time, but it was because I realized just how talented she was and wanted to push her to her full potential. It was never my intention to hurt her. You have a remarkable daughter," Gabriel spoke in earnest. Turning to Amy, he said, "I'll talk to you later." With that, he left the two women at the gazebo.

Amy watched his retreating figure disappear into the night before turning accusatory eyes on her mother. "How could you embarrass me like that?" she asked, throwing her hands up.

"I was saving you from making a mistake," Trish reasoned.

"And what mistake is that? Hmm?" Amy quirked a brow.

Trish released a heavy breath. "Amy, you just got out of an abusive relationship. Do you really think it is wise to get involved with someone now?"

Amy gave her mother an incredulous look. "You

haven't been my mother for twenty-one years, so what gives you the right to decide what's best for me now?"

Trish's eyes welled up with tears as she reached out to her daughter, her voice trembling. "Amy, please, you have to understand. I want to protect you. I couldn't protect you before, and I'm trying not to make the same mistakes again."

"You're such a hypocrite," Amy seethed as angry tears rolled down her cheeks. "How can you say you're trying to protect me when you're the one hurting me with all these secrets and keeping me at a distance? Did you even really want to find me?" Her vision blurred as the dam burst, and her heart squeezed tightly against her chest as she turned away.

Chapter Nineteen

"That's enough, you two." Nikki's voice broke through the tense silence that ensued after Amy's statement. Her voice rang with authority.

Trish wiped the tears staining her face to look at her sister, and Amy did the same.

"This pain you're both feeling is tearing you apart. But it doesn't have to be this way," Nikki continued, her face straining with concern.

"Trish, your daughter deserves to hear the truth about what happened," Nikki implored soothingly.

Trish's voice choked with emotion, managed to speak between sobs. "I never meant to hurt her. I love her so much."

"I know you do," Nikki replied, placing a comforting hand on her shoulder. "But Amy needs to hear it from you. She needs to understand why you made the decision to give her up for adoption all those years ago."

Trish slowly turned to her daughter. Amy gave her a

guarded look, even as the tears continued to stream down her face.

Trish extended her hands to her daughter in a desperate gesture. Her voice quivered with a mixture of determination and vulnerability. "It pains me I have hurt you this much," she said barely above a whisper, her voice laden with sorrow. "But I want to fix it. Please...let me fix it," she pleaded.

Amy's throat moved as she swallowed. Her blue eyes, reflective of her mother's, flickered with vulnerability. Her gaze soon transformed to one of determination as she finally spoke. "You need to tell me everything...or else I am leaving," she threatened.

Trish's heart accelerated as anxiety filled her. "I will. I promise." She nodded vigorously.

"I'll take care of wrapping up the party at the Nestled Inn." Nikki's voice rang through, reminding them she was still there. "You two can head over to the main house to talk."

The trio walked toward the inn; the sound of the party was still in full swing, getting louder the closer they got. Nikki headed inside, and Trish and Amy continued on to the main house. The silence was so thick. A million thoughts rushed through Trish's head as she fought the fear she could lose Amy forever this time, if she didn't tell her everything.

"Why don't we go to the living room," Trish suggested when they stepped through the front door.

"Okay," Amy automatically replied before walking in that direction.

Trish drew in a lungful of air before releasing it steadily through her open lips. Gathering her courage, she followed Amy.

Amy sat on the love seat, her hands clasped tightly in her lap, her back ramrod straight. Trish sat in the armchair facing her.

Trish took a deep breath, feeling the enormity of the moment. "Amy," she began, her voice laced with regret, "I'm so sorry. I should have told you everything from the start. I just... It was such a traumatic experience for me. I was young, and I didn't know how to handle it. I never thought about how I would explain it all to you when I finally found you."

"I never asked for this," Amy replied, her brows furrowed and her lips in a straight line. "I was okay with my life as it was, believing the people I called Mom and Dad were my actual parents and that I was just unlucky to be born into such a dysfunctional family. I was okay with that being my reality. But then all that changed... because of you. At first, I was angry, but then I became curious. I wanted to know who you were and why you decided I wasn't...worth it." Her voice cracked with pain as her gaze switched to a vulnerability that tore at Trish's soul.

Tears welled up in Trish's eyes as she mustered her courage. "I have always wanted you, Amy," she spoke in earnest.

"Then why did you give me up?"

Trish drew in a steadying breath. "Let me start from the beginning about how I met your father." She noted the curiosity her statement sparked in her daughter's eyes.

"His name was Frederick Laston," she said softly. "I met him at a party when I was just eighteen years old. He was six years older than me and a high school dropout. I thought he was the best thing to have happened in my life, and I fell hard. My parents didn't approve of him, especially your grandfather. He thought Frederick was nothing more than a tattooed hoodlum, and he believed I was disgracing our family by being with him."

"How did you end up pregnant with me?" Amy asked, breaking the silence that had fallen between them as Trish tried to gather the rest of her thoughts.

Trish sighed, her voice growing more somber. "I used to sneak out, and even lied that I was at my friends' place studying when I was really out with Frederick. It was an act of rebellion, a desperate attempt to hold on to something that felt real and exciting. But then, one day, everything changed."

She paused; her eyes clouded with memories. "The day I found out I got accepted into the university was the same day I discovered I was pregnant with you." She looked at her daughter with a bittersweet smile. "It was both the happiest and the scariest day of my life. I told Frederick, hoping he would stand by me. But instead, he told me he wasn't ready to have a child, and he stopped taking my calls and completely disappeared from my life."

Amy's face contorted with a mix of sadness and anger. "How could he do that? How could he just abandon you like that?"

Trish's voice wavered, tears welling in her eyes. "I don't have the answers, sweetheart. All I know is that I was left alone, scared, and uncertain about what the future held. I kept the pregnancy a secret from my parents for two whole months until I graduated from high school."

Silence hung in the air as Trish and Amy absorbed the weight of the revelation.

Trish took a deep breath, her voice quivering with

emotion as she continued her story. She looked into Amy's eyes, searching for understanding and forgiveness.

"You see, Amy," Trish began, her voice tinged with regret, "my parents had an enormous influence on my life. They were strict and controlling and had their own ideas about how I should live my life. My father," Trish continued, her voice trembling, "he threatened me. He said he would sue me for custody, claiming I was an unfit mother. And if I didn't terminate the pregnancy, I would no longer be welcome in their home."

Amy's expression became a mix of surprise and empathy. "I can't imagine how hard it must have been for you, Mom."

Trish rose from the chair and went over to crouch before Amy. Tentatively, she reached out, taking her hand in hers.

"Amy, I need you to believe me. Giving you up for adoption was the hardest decision I've ever made. I wanted to give you the best life possible, even if it meant sacrificing my own happiness. You were my greatest gift, and I wanted to ensure that you had the opportunities I couldn't provide at that time."

Amy's eyes filled with a mix of emotions—sadness, confusion, and compassion. "Why didn't you try to find me earlier?" she asked softly.

Trish's voice cracked as she answered, her words heavy with remorse. "I thought about you every day, Amy. But I was ashamed of what I had done, and I didn't know if you would want to know me. I didn't want to disrupt the life you had with your adoptive parents. I was afraid of being rejected. Never in my wildest dreams would I have thought you would have ended up in a home where you had to suffer the way you did."

Tears streamed down both their faces as the weight of their shared pain began to lift. Trish reached out to embrace her daughter, holding her tightly as they found solace in each other's arms.

"I'm so sorry, Amy," Trish whispered, her voice filled with genuine remorse. "I can't change the past, but I hope that one day, you can find it in your heart to forgive me."

* * *

Amy

"Amy! You made it."

"Hi, Sarah," Amy greeted just as the woman threw her arms around her shoulders. Amy's hands came up to hug her back. "I wouldn't miss little Buttercup's party for the world." She smiled at Sarah when they pulled apart. Sarah glowed like a sunbeam in a white, flowy dress that gave a slight glimpse of her bump and a bright smile to match her brown eyes. She had fast become so dear to Amy in such a short time.

"This is for you," Amy held up the small gift bag in her hand.

"Amy, you didn't have to do this," Sarah smiled appreciatively as she took the gift.

"I saw it and thought of you."

Sarah opened the bag and took out a white mug engraved with the words: I'm a Mom. What's your superpower? "Awe. I love this. Thank you so much," she expressed, drawing Amy in for another embrace.

"You're welcome," Amy returned.

Trish walked up to them just then and lightly touched Amy's arms. "Hi, Sarah. I just want to extend my congratulations to you and Aaron and pray for a healthy baby."

"Thanks, Trish. I appreciate it." Sarah smiled.

"Have you seen Nikki?" Trish asked.

"Last time I saw her, she was by the grill with Dad," Sarah replied.

"Okay, thank you," Trish replied before walking off.

"How are things between you two?" Sarah turned to ask when Trish was out of earshot.

"A whole lot better," Amy replied with an easy smile. "We had a good talk last week. I understand the situation a whole lot better now."

"That's great. I'm happy you guys are working it out," Sarah replied with a smile of her own as she lightly touched Amy's arm in support. "Would you excuse me for a bit? I need to talk to Aaron."

"That's okay," Amy assured her. "We'll catch up." Sarah left then.

Amy turned to appreciate the scene before her. Paul's backyard was a sprawling carpet of green, spacious and inviting, perfect for such an occasion. The setting was made all the more enchanting by the backdrop of the azure ocean, its hypnotic waves creating a soothing rhythm that blended with the laughter and chatter of the guests.

The yard was an explosion of pink and blue; the decorations hung like a collage of pastel clouds against the clear sky. Streamers fluttered in the breeze, their vibrant colors dancing in the sun. The table was laid with delectable cupcakes, their pink-and-blue frosting sparkling like tiny gemstones. An intriguing corner held a table strewn with cards and two large glass bowls. Guests could cast their predictions for the baby's gender.

"Hey, Nikki, how many burgers do you think I can flip at once?"

Her head swiveled in the direction of Paul's voice to see him by the grill. The scent of sizzling hamburgers wafted through the air.

"Paul, you better not ruin those burgers! I'm starving!" Nikki retorted, a playful scowl on her face, eliciting a chuckle from Paul. She walked over and stood by his side, and his free arm wrapped comfortably around her waist.

Her eyes found Aaron and Sarah then. Sarah's doting fiancé stood behind her, his hands massaging her back in a tender rhythm.

Amy's lips lifted in a smile at their tender display of affection.

"Are you enjoying yourself?"

She turned her head to see her mother standing beside her with a hopeful look.

"I am," she smiled. "It's beautiful," she spoke up, turning her head to take in everything.

"Yes, it is," Trish responded, her eyes soft with the sentiment. "This is a very special moment for them."

Sensing her mother's sadness, she reached over and gently touched her arm. Trish's gaze lifted to hers, and she gave her an encouraging smile, which she returned with an appreciative sweep of her lips. Ever since their heartfelt conversation, their bond had grown stronger.

As she continued to take in the scene before her, Amy's heart fluttered with a mix of emotions. It was a moment of reckoning, a realization that she was finally home. For most of her twenty-one years, she had wandered through life, a nomad searching for a place to belong. But now, surrounded by the love and support of Trish and their extended family, she finally felt a comforting sense of belonging that had eluded her for so long.

"So," Trish began, her voice gentle yet probing, "how's that young man? Gabriel, wasn't it?"

Amy's gaze shifted to her mother, a wistful smile tugging at the corners of her lips. "Gabriel... I haven't seen him in a week," she responded. "He had this culinary award thing in California. Said he'd be back next week."

She couldn't deny it—she missed him. They'd only spoken through texts since their almost kiss by the gazebo and him being in California. They had both stayed away from addressing it, but she was sure she hadn't been the only one who had felt the pull. She was going out of her mind with speculations about whether he regretted it.

Trish leaned closer; her voice filled with genuine concern. "Amy, I know it might not be my place, but I just want you to be careful. Your safety and happiness are all that matter to me."

Amy met her mother's gaze, her eyes shining with gratitude. "I appreciate your concern, Mom. I really do. But right now, Gabriel and I are just friends."

Trish nodded, her worry not entirely abated. "Are you sure about that? I mean, there's something more between you two, isn't there? I can see it in your eyes."

"All right, everyone, it's time."

Aaron's announcement saved her from answering a question for which she didn't have an answer.

"Are you ready?"

Aaron stood a few feet away, gripping a baseball bat tightly. He flashed a confident grin, adjusting his cap. "You bet!" he replied, his voice filled with determination. "I've got my game face on."

A ripple of excitement spread through the crowd as everyone gathered around, their eyes fixed on the expectant couple. Sarah stepped back, winding up her arm before hurling the baseball toward Aaron. The ball whizzed through the air, but Aaron swung his bat a fraction too late, missing the ball by a hair's breadth.

The guests burst into laughter and playful jeers, teasing Aaron for his near miss. Amy joined in the mirth, her laughter echoing through the air.

"Looks like you need some practice, honey!" Sarah teased, her eyes twinkling with amusement.

"Beginner's luck!" he called back, his voice laced with confidence. "Just watch this!"

Sarah readied herself for another throw. With a smirk, she pitched the baseball once more, and Aaron swung his bat. The ball sailed past him once again, the crowd erupting into laughter and cheers.

Aaron's face reddened with mock frustration, but he refused to give up. "Okay, okay," he conceded, chuckling. "Third time's the charm, right?"

The third throw came hurtling toward Aaron; everyone held their breath as he swung his bat. The crack of wood meeting leather resounded through the yard.

Poof!

The baseball burst open, revealing a cloud of pink dust. The crowd erupted into cheers and applause, their joyous voices blending with the sound of popping confetti cannons.

"It's a girl!" Sarah exclaimed, tears of joy streaming down her cheeks. Aaron enveloped her in a tight embrace.

Amy watched the scene unfold, her heart swelling with happiness for her friends.

Chapter Twenty

"Something smells amazing in here," Nikki's voice floated in from the doorway before she walked into the kitchen.

Trish slapped her hands rapidly against each other, attempting to lessen the layer of flour on them. The sweet aroma of freshly baked cookies enveloped the room, mingling with the comforting scent of vanilla.

"I'm baking apology cookies," she answered her sister's curious gaze.

"Apology cookies? For who?" Nikki quirked a brow.

"Reed," Trish replied with a sheepish smile.

Nikki's eyes sparkled with delight. "That's so thoughtful of you, Trish. I'm glad you're doing this. Reed means a lot to you, doesn't he?"

"He does," Trish said with an affirmative nod. "I just hope I haven't messed up our friendship too badly with all these unpredictable mood swings," she sighed as she wiped down the counter.

Nikki's folded lips curved up, and her lips were shown with empathy. "I'm sure it takes more than some mood swings to get rid of that man," she spoke assuredly.

Trish's eyes met her sister's, who stared back at her with a glint in their blue depths.

"That man loves you, Trish. You know that," she said plainly. 'The question is, will you let him?"

Trish's gaze slid to her hands flattened against the counter. "I'm scared," she confessed.

She didn't realize Nikki had moved until her palm covered the back of her hand. She lifted her eyes to see her sister's blue eyes filled with understanding and encouragement. "That's not a good enough excuse anymore."

Trish smiled tightly.

When she was finished baking, Nikki offered to drop her off, and she gratefully accepted.

Trish stepped through the entrance of the Humane Society, her hands clutching the vibrant container of freshly baked cookies and several boxes of dog biscuits. The air inside was filled with a medley of sounds—an occasional bark, a soft meow, and the rustling of paws against the linoleum floor. The scent of cleanliness mingled with the unmistakable aroma of animals, creating an atmosphere that was both comforting and lively.

Her eyes scanned the room, and her gaze settled on a sight that made her heart skip a beat. In a corner, bathed in light streaming through a nearby window, Reed knelt down next to a litter of tiny, mewling kittens. His hands moved with tenderness and grace as he gently stroked their fur, his touch radiating a deep affection for these vulnerable creatures.

Trish watched in awe as Reed's face lit up with a genuine smile, his eyes sparkling with a mixture of joy and contentment. It was evident he was in his element, a compassionate guardian to these innocent souls—one of the things she loved about him. The sight melted something within her, filling her with a warmth that spread from her chest to the tips of her fingers.

Suddenly, Reed's gaze lifted, and their eyes locked. Time seemed to stand still as he began walking toward her. Trish could feel her heart pounding against her chest, its rhythm quickening with each step he took. Her breath caught in her throat as she prepared herself to face him, ready to offer the apology she knew was long overdue.

"Hi." He smiled in greeting as he stopped a few inches before her.

"Hi," she replied softly, a shy smile playing at the corners of her lips. "I brought you these." She held up the items in her hands.

Reed turned toward her, his expression a mix of surprise and curiosity. "Cookies, huh?" he said, a hint of a smile playing at the corners of his lips.

"Apology cookies," she clarified.

Reed's eyes softened, his gaze lingering on her. "You didn't have to do that."

"I wanted to." She jumped up. "I'm sorry for the way I acted that day when you brought me home from my appointment. I shouldn't have snapped at you like that, and I've felt so terrible ever since." Her eyes flickered with regret before they fell to her feet.

"Apology accepted," Reed replied, shaking the container with the cookies. "Just seeing you here again is enough." Trish's gaze lifted to his already smiling face, his eyes filled with affection that caused a shiver to run up her spine. "I shouldn't have brought up you needing to see a therapist. At least not until you're ready."

Trish sighed; her voice laced with sarcasm. "Seems like my accident brought up more scars than the one I'm sporting on my face." Her hand instinctively reached up to touch the raised scar running from her hairline to just above her left eyebrow.

Reed gently intercepted her hand, his fingers brushing against the delicate strands of her hair. "You're still as beautiful as the first day I saw you," he said, his voice filled with affection.

Trish's breath caught in her throat. She stared into Reed's eyes, seeing the sincerity and love that radiated from him.

"Can we go somewhere to talk?" she asked.

"Yeah. We can go out back." He led her to the back of the building and toward the bench just under the oak tree.

They sat in silence for more than a minute as Trish tried to collect her thoughts. She took a deep breath, her voice quivering slightly as she began to open up about her past. "Reed, there's something I need to tell you," she started, her eyes fixed on a distant point as memories flooded back. "Remember I told you my parents made me give up Amy for adoption because they thought it would ruin my life?"

"Yes, I remember," he replied.

"There's more to it. My parents... they were so controlling, especially my father, Stuart. He wanted me to be his replacement, to carry on the family legacy as a renowned journalist. He did everything to make sure that happened."

Reed's brow furrowed with concern. "I'm not liking the sound of this, Trish. What did they do?"

A hint of bitterness crept into Trish's voice as she

continued, her gaze now focused on her tightly clasped hands. "My father considered Nikki a failure because she didn't follow in his footsteps. He had this vision of our family's name living on through me, and he would stop at nothing to make it happen."

Reed swallowed, his Adam's apple moving up and down as his hand resting on the bench between them folded into a tight fist.

Trish sighed, her voice tinged with a mix of frustration and sadness. "I tried to resist, to forge my own path, but it seemed futile. My father always found a way to manipulate me. He used every opportunity to remind me of my sister's perceived failure, making me believe I was the only hope for our family's reputation. After my pregnancy and having to give up Amy, I fell into a state of depression." Trish's eyes glistened with unshed tears as she recalled the painful memory.

The feel of Reed's hand closing around hers warmed her heart and pushed her to continue.

"I thought therapy was supposed to be a safe space, a sanctuary where I could share my pain, fears, and doubts. But somehow, everything I confided in my therapist found its way back to my father. He used my vulnerability against me, twisting my own words to pressure me into fulfilling his wishes."

Reed's hand gently applied pressure. "I can't imagine how betrayed you must have felt, Trish. I understand why you were so touchy about the therapy thing. That person broke your trust."

Trish nodded, grateful for Reed's understanding. "Exactly. It became increasingly hard to trust anyone, to believe there were professionals who genuinely cared about my well-being. I built walls around myself, shielding my deepest thoughts and desires, afraid they would be used as ammunition against me."

Silence enveloped them for a moment, the weight of Trish's revelations hanging heavy in the air. Reed squeezed her hand gently, his voice filled with unwavering support. "Trish, I want you to know that I'm here for you. I may not be a therapist, but I promise you that your secrets are safe with me. Whatever you face this time, I am willing to face it with you."

A flicker of hope danced in Trish's eyes as she looked at Reed, her voice filled with gratitude. "Hearing you say that means so much to me," she smiled appreciatively.

"There's more to the story," she spoke softly.

"I'm here. I'm not going anywhere. No matter what," he spoke encouragingly.

"I had an abusive ex-husband—Derek." She felt Reed stiffen beside her. "It wasn't physical. But the words he spoke to me felt like wounds, and they cut deep." A flicker of pain crossed her face. "Derek knew exactly how to chip away at my self-esteem, like a sculptor shaping a piece of clay. He made me feel small, inadequate, and unworthy of love."

"How long were you two married?" Reed's voice sounded unnaturally deep, and she could feel the anger radiating from him.

"Five years," she replied softly.

Reed's brow furrowed. "But why did you stay with him for so long? Why didn't you leave sooner?"

Trish looked down at her hands, her voice barely above a whisper. "I stayed because I believed his words. I thought I deserved the treatment he dished out. It took me a long time to realize I deserved so much more."

Reed's eyes shut as he took in deep breaths. When he

finally rested his eyes on her, they were filled with conviction. "Trish, you are incredible. You deserve all the love and happiness in the world."

A small smile tugged at the corners of Trish's lips, appreciating Reed's words of encouragement. "Thank you. When I finally found the strength to divorce Derek, it was like a dam burst inside me. It opened up a whole new world of self-love and self-discovery. I discovered hobbies that brought me joy, like painting and hiking. I decided to move from the place that held so many painful memories, and that's when I came here and fell in love with the inn and bought it. Slowly but surely, I began to believe in myself again."

Reed's eyes gleamed with admiration. "That's remarkable, Trish. You are incredibly strong."

Trish blushed, grateful for Reed's support. "It hasn't been easy, but it was worth it. I was happy." Her voice wavered, a hint of sadness seeping into her words. "And then came the accident. It took away so much from me, Reed. It stole my independence, my mobility, and shattered the newfound confidence I had built."

Trish swallowed hard; her gaze fixed on her lap. "I'm...I'm afraid of losing our friendship," she admitted, her words barely a whisper. "I've been feeling so confused lately, and I don't want to ruin what we have."

Reed reached out and gently lifted her chin, forcing her to meet his gaze. "Trish, I care about you more than you know," he said softly. "Our friendship means the world to me. I love you, but I cherish what we have even more. I want to be there for you, to support you, and to help you heal. Losing you as a friend is not an option."

Trish's eyes welled up with tears, grateful for his honesty and understanding. "I care for you too, Reed—a lot," she smiled. "And I do want to see where this thing between us goes."

A glimmer of hope flickered in his gray eyes.

"But can we take it slow?"

Reed nodded, a small smile playing at the corners of his lips. "Of course, Trish. We'll take it as slowly as you need. I'm here for you, no matter what."

A surge of relief washed over Trish as she realized she didn't have to face her struggles alone. She took a deep breath and mustered the courage to share her next step.

Her lips lifted into a broad smile as her eyes filled with affection.

"I've... I've booked my first therapy session," she revealed, her voice trembling with a mix of vulnerability and determination. "I want to start healing, and I thought... maybe you could drive me?"

Reed's eyes softened, his hand still holding hers, giving it a squeeze. "Absolutely," he replied without hesitation.

Chapter Twenty-One

"Good morning, everyone. I hope you all had a productive week."

The door swung open, and a rush of cool autumn air swept into the room, causing a few stray strands of Amy's blond hair that hadn't been secured under her chef's hat to dance around her face. Her heart skipped a beat as Gabriel walked in, his presence commanding attention. The room seemed to brighten as he smiled and greeted the students. When his emerald eyes landed on her and lingered a bit longer, her heart picked up speed. It amazed her at how affected she was by just a stare, but she had missed him. It had been nearly two weeks since he'd gone to California. She guessed absence did make the heart grow fonder.

"Next week will be my last week as your guest lecturer. But I am proud of all the work we have accomplished. You have been exceptional students who have performed remarkably well under pressure and duress," Gabriel announced, his gaze finding Amy once more. "Before we begin, I wanted to remind you all about the practical exam coming up at the end of next week. The theme is to showcase what you do best as an aspiring pastry chef. I want you to wow me with your creations."

A buzz of excitement filled the room as the students started discussing among themselves what they would be making for their final piece.

"So, what's the deal between you and Gabriel?" Jill's voice interrupted Amy's thoughts.

Amy's heart slammed against her chest. Taking in a few calming breaths, she turned and looked at her friend, her brows furrowed. "What do you mean?"

"Oh, come on, Amy," Jill exclaimed in a frustrated whisper, ensuring their other classmates weren't hearing their conversation.

"I've seen the way he looks at you when he thinks no one's watching and the way you look at him too. You're in love with him, aren't you?" she asked seriously.

"We're just friends," Amy deflected.

Jill's eyes became saucers, and her mouth hung open. "I knew there was something going on between you two. When did this happen?" she asked when she'd recovered from the initial shock.

Amy released a nervous breath. "A month ago, he came by the restaurant while I was waitressing, and we spoke. He confessed he only pushed me the way he did because he saw my potential. We've been friends ever since."

Jill nodded contemplatively. "It all makes sense now."

"What does that mean?" Amy asked, feeling defensive.

"I mean, he was such an ogre to you, and I couldn't understand it because you're better than most of us in this class, and yet you were the one publicly singled out for criticism. I noticed when he stopped being mean to you and started praising your work, you became less stressed," Jill expressed.

"Please don't tell anyone. I don't need anyone thinking I'm getting special favors just because we're friends now," Amy pleaded.

"Amy, come on. We're friends. I would never do that to you," Jill defended.

Amy gave her friend a grateful smile, and the two women returned to working on their practical pieces.

"I still think he likes you though," Jill sidled up to her ten minutes later and whispered.

"Jill, come on. I'm trying to concentrate," Amy playfully huffed while her heart beat rapidly against her chest.

"I think you like him too," her friend continued, undeterred with a knowing expression.

"Maybe I do," she finally confessed with a small smile of her own.

Jill's eyes widened before a triumphant grin lifted her lips. "You go, girl," she cheered and returned to her station.

Amy chuckled while shaking her head. She returned to her work undeterred for the next forty-five minutes.

After the class had ended, Amy's classmates bustled through the door and made their way to their other classes.

"Amy, could you stay back for a moment? I'd like to talk to you." Gabriel stopped her before she could exit the class.

Jill looked back at her with a knowing grin before she left.

When they were finally alone, Gabriel walked over to her station, where Amy stood rigid, her heart pounding.

"Congratulations on your award," she said, breaking the awkward silence.

"Thank you." Gabriel smiled, his eyes shining like jewels.

"How was California?"

"California was great. I had a wonderful time. I only wish my parents could have been there to see me collect my award, but they live all the way in London."

"Gabriel, I'm sure your parents are proud of you, no matter where they are," Amy said.

"I still wished I could have shared that moment with someone special." Gabriel's eyes locked with hers, and for a moment, the world around them faded away. Amy's heart raced, and her mind filled with a whirlwind of emotions. She couldn't deny the connection that had blossomed between them, the unspoken chemistry that lingered in the air.

"Amy, I wanted to talk to you about something important," he began after their charged stare-off, his voice low and tinged with vulnerability. He ran a hand through his brown locks, a nervous habit she had come to find endearing.

"I'm leaving in two weeks—after Thanksgiving," he revealed.

Amy's eyes widened, a mixture of surprise and disappointment washing over her. "Oh, okay."

Gabriel's lips folded and lifted slightly. "I have to head back to New York," he further explained, "I've been away from my restaurant for too long now."

"Well, I hope you don't forget me. You can shoot me a text now and again," Amy spoke, inflecting as much cheeriness as she could muster, even though his words felt like a punch in the gut.

Gabriel's expression became serious. "There's something I've been meaning to talk to you about, Amy. I've been meaning to do so for some time now." He threaded a hand through his hair.

Amy held her breath, her body tensing as she waited for him to continue.

"I want to be honest with you, Amy. I've grown fond of you, more than I can put into words. I enjoy spending time with you."

"I enjoy spending time with you too." The words rushed from her lips.

His eyes abruptly fell to the floor, and an audible gulp filled the silence before his gaze drifted up to her face. A myriad of emotions flashed in their emerald depths—nervousness, determination, and one that caused her to take in a sharp breath.

"I like you, Amy—a lot. I've been interested in you from the first day, but I didn't want to cross a line, being that I was your instructor. I tried to stay away, to keep you at a distance—maybe that's part of the reason I was so hard on you." He chuckled.

Amy stared at him bug-eyed, a hand pressed against her throat as she listened to him confess his feelings for her.

"But no matter how hard I tried, I couldn't stay away or keep you out of my mind. Spending time with you, even just as friends, has been the highlight of my time here. Back in California, all I thought about was how much I missed you—your smile, your kindness, and your courage."

"So, what are you saying?" she asked in a whisper.

"Amy, I would like to have a relationship with you—

that's if you're interested in me too," he answered, his tone hopeful.

A smile split her face at her uncontained joy as her heart swelled. The realization that Gabriel felt the same way sent a jolt of warmth through her veins. She took a step closer to him. "I like you too, Gabriel," she confessed, her voice barely above a whisper. "A lot," she added, which garnered a chuckle from him. The sound felt like music to her ears and brought a warmth she didn't realize she needed until that moment.

"How does this work?"

A soft smile played on Gabriel's lips, and he reached out to gently brush her cheek. "Would you be willing to give a long-distance relationship a chance? I can't promise it'll be easy, but I believe in us, in what we have."

Amy's eyes searched his, her heart fluttering with a mix of hope and uncertainty. She took a deep breath, her voice steady. "Yes. I want to give this a chance. We'll make it work, won't we?"

Gabriel's smile widened, his eyes sparkling with affection. He pulled her into an embrace, his warmth enveloping her. "We will," he spoke with conviction.

"There's one more thing I need to tell you," he said when they separated.

"More earth-shattering than you confessing your feelings?" Amy quirked a brow as a smirk played on her lips.

"Not quite, but it is something," he replied with an easy grin. "A friend of mine reached out about us partnering and opening a restaurant in Oak Harbor."

Amy's blue eyes widened in surprise. "Oak Harbor? That's incredible!"

Gabriel nodded in agreement. "If we get the green

light, I would be motivated to maybe spend half my time in New York and the next half here."

"That would be awesome." Amy smiled.

"I'm going out there tomorrow to check out the site. You have the day free; want to come with me?" he offered.

"Are you asking me on a date?" Amy asked, a glint in her eyes.

Gabriel's gaze softened as a smile tugged at the corners of his mouth. "I suppose I am. So will you accompany me, my fair lady?"

Amy giggled. "I shall, kind sir," she responded, placing her hand in his extended one. Gabriel brought her hand up to his lips and placed a delicate kiss there. Warmth spread from the pit of her stomach all over her body.

* * *

"You know," Gabriel's voice broke the silence. He and Amy had been traveling for the past half hour as they made their way to Oak Harbor. "Oak Harbor is a lot like Camano. It's got some fantastic hiking trails, and the scenery"—he gestured out the window with a sweeping motion—"is something to marvel at."

Amy had to agree with him. The highlight of the trip so far was the majestic Deception Pass, where emerald waters churned beneath a grand bridge, and landforms jutted out of the water like the back of some ancient, submerged beast. "It's like a beautiful painting come to life," she replied, drinking in the magnificence.

Soon, they were greeted by the welcome sign of the town—a rustic wooden placard adorned with intricate carvings of the local flora and fauna. The sign stood like a sentinel amidst a backdrop of verdant fields, a picturesque skyline, and distant mountains that stood like stoic guardians.

"I love it already," Amy confessed, her eyes sparkling brighter than the morning star. "There's something so... welcoming about this place."

"I agree," Gabriel nodded, keeping his eyes on the road as they drove through the town.

The car finally rolled to a halt in front of a grand old building that stood proudly near the waterfront. Gabriel led Amy toward it, his steps purposeful, a gleam of excitement in his eyes. The view of the Cascade Mountains from the building was breathtaking, with their towering peaks dusted with snow, standing sentinel over the town and the tranquil waters.

A man, tall and well-built, detached himself from the shadows of the building and walked toward them. His grin was infectious as he clapped Gabriel on the shoulder, his gaze flitting to Amy.

"Gabriel, I'm so happy you could make it."

"Hi, Jacob," Gabriel greeted. "This is Amy." He stepped to the side, making her more visible to the man.

"Nice to meet you, Amy," Jacob said.

"Nice to meet you too, Jacob," she returned, taking the hand he held out to her.

Jacob turned to Gabriel, a look of mischief in his brown eyes. "You did good," he smiled wide. "Compared to your usual."

Gabriel's ears flashed pink, and he cleared his throat. "Why don't you show us the inside?" he asked.

Jacob led them toward the building, and Amy wondered what their earlier conversation had been about.

The day was filled with exploration, the state park

being the last stop. Gabriel and Amy, hand in hand, strolled along the shore of Deception Pass, the scent of hotdogs and sodas from the nearby stall wafting through the air. They settled on a park bench, the food in their hands a simple yet comforting meal.

Afterward, they continued their stroll along the shoreline of the Pass.

"This place...it's a treasure." Amy sighed appreciatively as they stared out at the wide expanse of the ocean and the landforms jutting out of the water, while birds hovered over the horizon.

"I am definitely opening the restaurant here," Gabriel spoke beside her.

She lifted her head to smile approvingly. "I think you should," she agreed.

As the sun began to set, a chill crept over the landscape, causing Amy to shiver. "Cold?" Gabriel, noticing, asked.

"It's a little chilly," she replied.

Shrugging out of his jacket, he gently draped it over her shoulders, his touch lingering as he pulled her closer.

"Thank you," she spoke softly as she brought the jacket tighter around her and nestled closer to him, relishing his masculine scent. They shared a moment of silence, their gazes locked on the scene before them.

Chapter Twenty-Two

Trish nervously twirled a strand of her sandy-blond hair around her finger as she stood before the mirror. The soft glow of the vanity lights illuminated the room, casting a warm, flattering light on her face. Nikki stood beside her, a vibrant smile on her lips as she held a makeup brush poised in her hand.

"You're going to knock him off his feet, Trish," Nikki assured her, her voice dripping with enthusiasm. "Reed won't be able to take his eyes off you."

Trish offered a weak smile, her blue eyes flickering with doubt. "I hope so. But my scar...it's all I can see," she said barely above a whisper.

Nikki placed a comforting hand on her shoulder. "Sis, you are beautiful inside and out. That scar doesn't define you. It's just a part of your story, a reminder of how strong you are. Reed knows that too. That man has seen you at your lowest, and his affection has remained unchanged. Just focus on the special bond that you two share," she encouraged, her eyes staring at her through the mirror with genuine affection.

Trish's gaze dropped to the makeup spread out on the vanity, her fingers tracing the edge of the concealer. With a deep breath, she picked up the brush and dabbed it gently onto her forehead, skillfully camouflaging the scar. As she examined her reflection, she could still see the faint ridge beneath the makeup, a constant reminder of the traumatic accident that had left its mark. Her hand came up to trace the outline of it.

"Trish, would you stop?" Nikki blew out a frustrated breath. "You're beautiful in every single way, so don't bring yourself down today."

Trish turned to her sister; her lips slightly lifted as she quirked a brow at her. "Did you just paraphrase Christina Aguilera's song to me?"

"You're darn right I did," Nikki affirmed, her blue gaze determined. "And that's the truth. You are beautiful. Stop focusing on the things that don't matter."

Trish nodded before turning back to the mirror. She bit her lip, her gaze lingering on her reflection. She wanted to believe Nikki's words and find solace in her unwavering support. Taking a deep breath, she closed her eyes and repeated the mantras she had learned in therapy, the words becoming a shield against her doubts.

"I am enough, worthy of friendship and love, just as I am," she whispered, her voice gaining strength. "My value is not diminished by my imperfections or the perceptions of others."

Nikki beamed; her voice filled with pride. "That's it, Trish! You've got this."

Trish opened her eyes, a newfound resolve shining in her gaze. She met Nikki's gaze, gratitude welling up within her.

When she had finished getting dressed, Trish stood before the full-length mirror in her bedroom, her sandy-blond hair now cascading down her shoulders. The sapphire dress she wore accentuated her figure well, and her blue eyes shimmered with a mix of excitement and apprehension.

As she made her way to the door, Trish turned to Nikki, a genuine smile gracing her lips. "Wish me luck."

Nikki returned the smile, her eyes glittering with excitement. "You don't need luck, Trish. You're a radiant force of nature. Reed won't stand a chance."

Trish descended the stairs, her heart pounding with anticipation. As she reached the bottom, her eyes met Reed's, and she couldn't help but notice the surprise that flickered across his face. His mouth dropped open, a mixture of astonishment and admiration, while his eyes sparkled with adoration. A warm smile spread across Trish's face as Reed's lips gently brushed against her cheek, followed by the back of her hand, an affectionate gesture that sent a shiver of delight through her.

"You look absolutely stunning," Reed murmured, his voice filled with genuine admiration. "I'm the luckiest man in the world to be in your presence tonight."

Trish blushed, feeling a rush of warmth surge to her cheeks. "Thank you, Reed. You look rather dashing your-self," she returned his compliment, taking in his neatly fitted gray slacks and blazer that showed off his broad shoulders, his lean but muscular physique. His blue turtleneck made it clear he worked out as it stretched across his chest and tapered to his waist. Black loafers completed his outfit. His low-cut brown hair, clean-shaven face, and brilliant gray eyes made him look like he could be on the cover of *GQ*.

"These are for you." He lifted the bouquet of red-and-white roses.

"Oh, thank you. These are beautiful." Trish smiled as she took them from him. She couldn't help but bury her nose in their velvety petals, inhaling the soft fragrance they produced.

"Not as beautiful as you," Reed returned, causing her cheeks to flush with warmth as she blushed—although she wasn't sure they had returned to their natural hue since he arrived.

"I'll take those," Nikki's voice interrupted their moment to say.

Trish looked over her shoulder to see her sister at the foot of the stairs, her eyes gleaming. Turning, she placed them in her outstretched hand.

Amy came from the kitchen just then. "Wow! Mom, you look stunning," she exclaimed, giving Trish an appreciative once-over.

"Thank you, sweetie," Trish smiled appreciatively.

"Hi, Reed. You look good too." Amy shifted her gaze to the man standing beside Trish.

"Thank you, Amy." Reed chuckled.

"You kids have fun now. Reed, you know the rule. Don't bring her back until she's had a blast," Nikki instructed with a smirk.

Reed chuckled at this. "You got it." He extended his arm, offering it to Trish. "Shall we?"

Trish gracefully looped her hand through his and allowed him to guide her outside. Her eyes widened in surprise as they descended the porch steps. Instead of his truck, a white Mercedes Benz GLE Coupe. The car screamed luxury. As Reed helped her into the passenger side, she couldn't help but melt into the plush leather seat.

Thirty minutes later, they passed through Arlington, then through Marysville, and another thirty minutes later, they were in Seattle.

As Reed drove along the waterfront, the iconic Space Needle pierced the darkened sky, its illuminated presence a beacon in the night. Skyscrapers towered above, their windows radiating a kaleidoscope of colors. The streets were alive with activity as people strode along the sidewalks. It was electric.

They finally came to a stop before a building whose architecture was a blend of modern and classic charm. It was adorned with large windows that allowed streams of soft, warm light to spill onto the bustling streets.

As Reed helped her out of the car, Trish couldn't help but gape at it all. A valet came just then, and Reed handed him his car key before escorting Trish inside.

Soft music greeted them upon entrance, as well as polished marble floors and a magnificent chandelier hanging from the lofty ceiling in the middle of the room.

"Good evening. Welcome to La Belle Cuisine. My name is Samantha. How may I direct you?" a woman dressed in a straight black dress with a tag attached greeted her with a friendly smile.

"Good evening," Reed greeted back. "Reservations for Hastings," he informed her.

The woman's eyes flipped to the tablet lying on the podium before her. Her finger moved over the screen as her brows drew together in concentration. "Oh, yes. Reed Hastings. Your table has already been prepared," she confirmed, walking from behind the podium and leading them through the room.

Trish used the time to whisper, "Reed, just how rich are you? This place is like something out of a fairy tale."

Reed chuckled as he turned to look down at her. His eyes twinkled in the soft glow of the hanging lights. "Let's just say I enjoy treating you to the best, my dear. Tonight is all about you."

Trish's cheeks reddened even as an automatic smile graced her lips.

As they settled into their private corner, Reed's gaze never wavered from Trish. "Tonight, I only want my eyes on you," he confessed, his voice filled with sincerity. "And I hope to have the privilege of seeing your gaze fixed upon me as well. You have my undivided attention."

Trish felt her heart skip a beat at his words. She had never experienced such an undeniably intense connection with someone before. "Reed, I know I said we should take things slow, and this is just...wow," she exclaimed.

"Is it too much?" Reed asked, his gray eyes filling with concern.

"No, no. That's not what I'm saying," she rushed to put his mind at ease. "I've never felt so seen and cherished before. Thank you."

Reed smiled then, the action causing his gray eyes to crinkle at the corners. It was so sincere—so endearing. Her lips lifted in a similar way.

The waiter, a young man with a friendly smile, approached their table, offering them menus.

"What would you recommend?" Trish asked the waiter, eyes scanning the menu.

"The duck confit is a house specialty, ma'am. And the chocolate soufflé for dessert is quite remarkable," he replied.

"That sounds perfect," she said, handing her menu back. Reed nodded at the waiter, indicating he'd have the same.

As the waiter retreated, Reed and Trish began a dance of conversation that spanned from the mundane to the profound. Reed's voice softened as he spoke of his late wife, Laura. "She was a neurosurgeon, you know, one of the best," he said, a note of pride seeping into his voice. "The irony of it all...she, a brain surgeon, taken by a brain tumor."

Trish's heart clenched at his words, and she reached out, her hand covering his. "How long ago was this?"

"Twelve years."

"I'm so sorry, Reed," she said, her voice barely more than a whisper. "That's a cruel twist of fate."

Reed nodded, his eyes distant. But then he looked at Trish, his gaze softening. "You remind me of Laura in some ways," he admitted, his eyes brimming with a mix of nostalgia and something more. "But there's so much more about you that I find lovable. You have a spirit, a radiance that is truly yours, and I am honored I get to experience it."

A rush of warmth flooded Trish's cheeks as she smiled. "I'm honored to have a place in your heart alongside the memories of Laura."

Their first course arrived just then, a beautifully presented salad with crisp greens and vibrant dressings; then came the main course. Trish couldn't help but marvel at the taste that exploded in her mouth with each bite. It was a sensory experience that matched the depth of their conversation.

Internally, Trish felt a whirlpool of emotions. She felt empathy for the man who had loved and lost so deeply yet found the courage to love again. She felt a certain fear too —of being compared, of being a replacement. But more than anything, she felt a burgeoning affection for Reed, a man who, despite his past, was looking at her with such sincere love. She realized she was ready to be loved by him, ready to make new memories to replace the pain and darkness of the past.

Trish raised a questioning brow when Reed rose from his chair and held out a hand to her. "May I have this dance?" he asked, a gentle smile gracing his lips.

Trish's heart soared, and she nodded, her hand finding its place in his. They moved together in perfect harmony, their bodies swaying to the rhythm of the soft music floating from the speakers. The world around them faded into insignificance as they lost themselves in the embrace of the music.

"While we're taking it slow, is it okay for me to say, Trish, you take my breath away?" Reed whispered softly, his voice laced with genuine admiration, before pulling back to look at her now blushing face.

"I'll allow it." She smiled demurely up at him.

Reed's hand found its way to Trish's cheek, his touch tender and full of longing. Their gazes locked, and time stood still as their lips met in a gentle, heartfelt kiss. It was a kiss that spoke of promises and shared dreams, sealing their connection in a moment of pure bliss.

Chapter Twenty-Three

Trish eagerly waited on her porch, her heart fluttering with anticipation as she watched Reed's truck pull up in front of her house. The sound of the engine reverberated in the silence of the early morning. Reed stepped out of the vehicle, a warm smile spreading across his face as he caught sight of Trish.

"Hey there," Reed greeted, his voice filled with genuine warmth as he walked onto the porch. Trish readily fell into his waiting arms, welcoming the instant warmth that surrounded her as she snuggled into his chest. "Ready for our little adventure?" he asked when they separated, his eyes bright with excitement.

Trish nodded, her eyes sparkling with a mix of nervousness and exhilaration. "Definitely. I've been looking forward to this."

"Well, I do hope this date will be up there with our date last week." His voice was hopeful.

"All that matters is getting to spend time with you, whether it's at expensive restaurants or just working alongside you at the Society; I'm happy," Trish assured him, planting a kiss on his cheek.

Reed's lips parted in a grin. "Well then, let's make this a day to remember—together."

Trish climbed into the passenger seat, the comforting scent of leather filling her senses as she settled in. Reed started the engine, and they set off down the road, with the truck's tires humming against the asphalt.

"So, where are we headed?" Trish asked, breaking the silence that had enveloped them.

Reed's smile widened. "First, we're going for a long drive. I'm taking the scenic route through Camano Island. Trust me; you're going to love it."

Trish nodded; her gaze fixated on the road ahead. As they turned onto Camano Hill Drive, she couldn't help but feel a sense of liberation. The wind tousled her hair, and she inhaled deeply, savoring the crisp air that filled her lungs. The late autumn landscape painted the surroundings with hues of orange, red, and gold, as nature itself was preparing for the holiday season.

After a while, Trish mustered the courage to speak. "Reed, I wanted to tell you something."

His eyes flicked toward her briefly before returning to the road. "What is it?" he asked, his tone encouraging.

A hint of vulnerability tinged her voice as she continued, "I want to thank you for all the support you've given me since my accident. You've played such a major part in my recovery. Dealing with my PTSD hasn't been easy, but you've been there for me every step of the way. The thought of you and my family supporting me through this time has been a source of strength to me, and I am deeply grateful."

Reed's hand gently reached for hers, intertwining their fingers.

"I'm glad I could be there for you. You're strong, and you've come so far. I'm honored to be your knight in shining armor, if that's what you see me as," he spoke fondly.

Trish smiled, a warmth spreading through her chest. "You're more than that, Reed. You form an important piece of my anchor that keeps me tethered."

He lifted their intertwined hands to his lips and kissed the back of her hand. Warmth spread from the spot and traveled up her arm until she was fully blushing.

A comfortable silence settled between them, their unspoken emotions filling the truck's cabin. Trish's fear had gradually diminished over time, and it was now replaced by a newfound sense of trust. She yearned to take control, to prove to herself she could overcome her anxieties.

"Reed, would you mind if I drove for a while?" Trish asked, her voice brimming with determination.

Reed's eyebrows shot up in surprise, but he quickly recovered, a proud smile playing on his lips. "Of course. If that's what you want," he spoke encouragingly before pulling over to the side of the road.

With a surge of confidence, Trish slid into the driver's seat as Reed adjusted it to fit her stature. Familiarizing herself with the controls, she drew in a deep, steadying breath and released it before turning the key. The engine roared to life once again as she grasped the steering wheel tightly. Her hands were steady, despite the adrenaline coursing through her veins. With another deep breath, she released the brake, and the truck jerked forward, startling her. She quickly slammed her foot back down, causing the vehicle to stop.

"Remember, Trish," Reed said, his voice steady and reassuring. "You're stronger than you think. I'm right here with you." Trish nodded; her gaze fixed on the road ahead. Slowly, she released the brake once more. The truck slowly rolled onto the asphalt before going at a steady pace.

As they continued their journey through the countryside, Trish couldn't help but revel in the freedom she felt. Reed directed her toward the Kristofferson farm.

"You know, for as long as I've lived here, I've only visited here once, and it was in the summer," Trish revealed. "It was a wonderful experience. I don't know why I didn't make it back here."

"Well then, you're going to love how different it looks for the season," Reed turned and grinned knowingly.

When they drove through the gates, the air was alive with the scents of pine and cinnamon, while the farm's buildings were strung with a tapestry of pepper lights that were sure to sparkle at night. Trish's eyes lit with anticipation as she took in the merry sights around her.

As they stepped through the entrance, Trish's eyes widened with delight. The farm's holiday open house was in full swing, bustling with visitors. The main barn had been transformed into a cozy gathering space filled with laughter and conversation.

"Hi. Welcome to Kristofferson's. I'm Kaley, and we're happy to have you," a bright-faced girl who looked to be in her late teens greeted them and handed them each a steaming cup of spiced cider and a plate of freshly baked cookies.

Trish savored the sweet warmth of the cider. "Mmm,

this is just what I needed on a chilly day like today," she said, taking a bite of a gingerbread cookie.

Reed nodded in agreement, his lips curling into a smile. "Nothing like a cup of hot cider to warm you up from the inside out.

As they indulged in their treats, they noticed the inviting wine-tasting area nearby. Curiosity piqued, they made their way over, where a vintner stood behind a rustic wooden table, pouring samples of their finest local wines.

"Welcome!" the vintner greeted them with a smile. "Please, take your time and sample our selection."

Trish and Reed exchanged glances; their eyes alight with excitement. They swirled the wine in their glasses, inhaling the rich aromas before taking delicate sips.

"Mmm, this red wine has such a velvety texture," Trish commented, savoring the flavors on her palate. "And the white wine is so crisp and refreshing."

Reed nodded in agreement, his eyes twinkling. "Yeah, the winemakers on this island truly have a talent for crafting exceptional wines." After purchasing a bottle of their favorite wine, they continued their adventure through the farm.

Trish and Reed meandered through the farm's gift shop, their eyes wandering over the array of unique hand-crafted items and festive decorations. Trish picked up a delicate ceramic ornament, admiring its intricate design.

"I think this would look great on my mantle," she spoke appreciatively.

Reed reached into his pocket and fished out a few bills before walking up to the store clerk.

"We'd like to purchase that piece," he said, pointing to the ornament in Trish's hands.

Trish's lips fell open before she closed them and walked over to him. "You really don't have to buy me anything. I was just thinking out loud," she spoke.

Reed smiled down at her, determination shining through his gray eyes. "I know, but I want to buy it for you."

Trish ran her tongue across her lips. "Thank you," she said softly.

"It was my pleasure." He smiled back.

As they explored farther, they stumbled upon a bustling craft workshop where participants were engrossed in creating their own holiday wreaths. Trish's eyes sparkled with delight.

"Can we join the workshop? I've always wanted to learn how to make my own wreath."

Reed chuckled; his voice filled with warmth. "You have?"

Trish eagerly nodded like a kid being offered candy. "Absolutely."

"Let's do it then. Let's embrace our creative sides together," he agreed.

They joined the workshop, selecting fresh cuttings from the forest. Trish reveled in the natural fragrance that enveloped them. Her nimble fingers wove the foliage into a beautiful wreath adorned with vibrant ribbons and aromatic pinecones.

As they completed their wreaths, a fellow workshop participant turned to them with a smile. "Your wreaths are stunning! They will be the perfect centerpiece for your holiday decorations."

Trish's lips turned up in an unsure smile before she looked at Reed. He wore an impish grin, his eyes swimming with mischief.

"Thank you so much. We will definitely consider using it as our centerpiece," he answered the woman. Trish's cheeks turned crimson, and then, as she ducked her head, warmth emanated from her chest.

As the afternoon waned, Reed escorted Trish back to the truck and helped her into the passenger side before settling back into the driver's seat. The amber hues of the setting sun cast a warm glow over them and the countryside as he drove her back to the house.

"Reed, I had the most incredible time today," she confessed when they were standing on her porch.

"I did too," Reed agreed, his eyes fixed on her and filled with affection. "I love you, Trish," he spoke with heartfelt emotion.

Trish's gaze softened as her heart beat wildly against her chest. "I love you too, Reed," she finally said the words. Reed's gray eyes filled with joy as his head descended until their lips were connected.

She walked into the house feeling like she was on cloud nine, wearing a wide grin.

"Oh, someone's happy." Nikki cocked her head to the side with a raised brow as she stared at her sister from the stool around the kitchen island.

"How was your date with Reed, Mom?" Amy asked from the stove where she stood, stirring a pot.

"It was wonderful," Trish sighed happily. "We went to the Kristofferson Farm, did a wine tasting, bought a few things, and crafted wreaths." She held up her creation, along with a gift bag and her other items.

"Ooh, let me see," Nikki said, sliding off the chair and walking up to her. She took the bag from Trish, removing the bottle of wine and the ornament she'd gotten. "These look pricey." She nodded in approval.

"They were," Trish chuckled. "But Reed insisted on getting them for me."

"Classy man. I approve." Nikki smiled broadly.

"Kristofferson Farm, that's the one on NE Camano Drive, right?" Amy asked, looking over her shoulder.

"Yeah, that's right," Trish answered.

"Gabriel wanted to visit there before he leaves next week. He wanted to sample their wine too, to see if they'd be a good fit for the new restaurant."

Trish's smile waned, and her stomach knotted with concern. She crossed the room to stand beside her daughter. "This smells great," she complimented. "What are you making?"

"Lentil stew,' Amy replied.

"It smells heavenly." Trish placed her hand around her shoulders. "My daughter, the chef," she proudly stated. Amy leaned her head against her shoulder. "You know," she began, her voice tinged with concern, "I worry about you, Amy. I don't want you to take it the wrong way, but I would lose my mind if something ever happened to you. After what Jake did to you, I just want you to be careful." Her eyes pleaded.

Amy smiled softly; her eyes filled with understanding. "I get where you're coming from, Mom. But I need you to understand that Gabriel is different. He's kind and caring, and I genuinely believe his intentions are pure."

Nikki chimed in then, "Paul actually vouched for Gabriel. He said he's a stand-up guy, someone we can trust."

Trish's worry lines deepened, but she realized she had to trust Amy's judgment. "Well, if Paul says he's a good guy, then that carries some weight. But promise me, Amy, that you'll always be cautious and listen to your instincts."

Amy nodded, her determination shining through. "I will."

The room fell silent for a moment, as if everyone was contemplating the weight of the conversation.

"There's something I wanted to talk to you about," Amy spoke up, turning off the stove and turning fully to Trish.

"Shoot," Trish encouraged.

"I want to find my biological father."

Trish's heart clenched with a mix of fear and anticipation. She knew the journey to uncovering the truth could be rocky and emotionally draining, but she also understood the importance of closure.

"I won't lie, Amy," Trish said, her voice filled with a blend of trepidation and support. "I am fearful that what you find might hurt you, but you deserve closure for this chapter of your life, and I will support you in any way I can."

Nikki's eyes darted between Trish and Amy, and there was apprehension in her eyes as well. "You're brave, Amy. And we'll be right there beside you every step of the way." She threw in her support.

Amy's face lit up with a mixture of gratitude and determination. "Thank you, both of you. I really appreciate it." She hugged her mother before walking over to Nikki and doing the same.

Trish watched her daughter with pride at the strength and bravery she possessed. She admired her will to take chances, even though she had been hurt so many times. Still, she couldn't help but feel a surge of apprehension for what lay ahead for her daughter in trying to find Frederick.

Chapter Twenty-Four

"I'm sorry."

Amy's chest tightened at the gravity of the private investigator's voice.

"Frederick Laston passed away in a car crash ten years ago." Greg slid over a printout of an obituary, the melancholic words forming a portrait of a man she would never meet. "It says he was survived by a daughter and his parents." Amy felt a wave of disappointment washing over her.

"I wish it were better news, but that's all that I was able to find on the man. If you'd like information on his parents and his daughter, I can look into it for you," Greg continued, his tone apologetic.

Amy couldn't find the words to answer him as she looked at the picture of the man who was her biological father, the source of half her genes, and a ghost of the past. She would never meet him, never hear his voice, never get the closure she so desperately craved.

"Thanks, Greg. This was helpful," Trish spoke up instead. "We'll call you and let you know what she's decided." She rose from the wicker chair she had been sitting on and held out her hand to the gentleman, who also stood before taking her hand.

"Okay, Trish. I'll look out for your call." With that, he walked off the porch, got into his car, and left.

"Talk to me, Amy," Trish implored gently, her calm voice ringing through the storm of emotions churning within Amy.

"I don't...I don't know what to say," Amy looked up at her mother, eyes reflecting her vulnerability.

"Pretend I am him. What would you have wanted to say to him if you had met him?" Trish asked.

Amy released a heavy breath. Her eyes welled up as she gathered her thoughts. "I would have asked him, why didn't he want me?" she confessed, her voice breaking as she stared at her mother with glistening eyes. "How could he have left you when you were pregnant and needed him the most? How could he have allowed you to make all those decisions alone? Why didn't he try to find me?"

With that, the dam of emotions within her broke. Tears streamed down her face as she grappled with the reality of her situation, the burden of her unhealed wounds making her heart heavier. The knowledge she had been given up for adoption, that she had been unwanted, was a wound that was still raw, still hurting.

"Oh, Amy," Trish whispered, pulling her into a comforting embrace. She let Amy cry, her tears soaking her shoulder as she apologized over and over again. "I am so sorry...so...so sorry. I wish I could have done things differently. I wish I had kept you all those years ago." As Amy cried, Trish held her tighter, their shared pain mingling in the silence.

"I'm gonna go. I have my final piece to finish at school today," Amy told her mother as they separated.

"Okay, sweetheart. I'll be here when you get back. We can talk then," Trish spoke with a reassuring smile. She leaned over and placed a gentle kiss against Amy's cheek. "I love you. You've got this."

"Thanks, Mom," Amy replied with a watery smile before leaving the house and getting into her car. When she made it to school, she checked her face in the mirror to ensure the evidence of her breakdown was gone and took a deep breath before exiting. She made her way down the hall toward the kitchen.

"Hey, Amy. Ready to wow these examiners?" Jill asked as she fell in step with her.

"Of course I am," Amy chuckled lightly. "Are you?" She quirked a brow at Jill.

"Born ready," Jill replied with a wide grin.

When they walked through the door, the kitchen was already awake with activity as students scurried around, their faces etched with concentration and determination. Amy quickly walked to her station to start prepping.

Many hours later, flour dusted the countertops, mixing bowls clinked, and the aroma of freshly baked pastries wafted through the air. Amy, her brow furrowed, stood at her station, delicately applying the finishing touches to her creation. Her hands moved with both precision and grace, a testament to her countless hours of practice. With each stroke of the spatula, the sugar icing transformed into intricate designs resembling delicate lace cascading down the cake's tiers.

"Great job, guys. You're doing so well." Gabriel's voice rang out over the sounds of the kitchen. Their eyes met, and Gabriel shot her a reassuring nod before turning his attention to a student in need.

"All right, everyone," Gabriel announced half an hour later, his voice resonating throughout the room. "Time's up! Put down your tools and step away from your final pieces."

Amy's heart raced as she stepped back from her masterpiece, her breath catching in her throat. The room brimmed with anticipation as Gabriel and Professor Reynolds moved from station to station, carefully examining each student's creation.

After what felt like an eternity, Professor Reynolds cleared his throat, capturing everyone's attention. "I have reviewed each and every one of your final exam pieces, and I must say, I am thoroughly impressed with the level of skill and creativity on display here today. Gabriel has been an exceptional tutor."

The class erupted in applause, and a small smile raised the corners of Gabriel's lips at the compliment.

"Now for your grades."

Amy waited with bated breath as Professor Reynolds called out everyone's grades. Her brows furrowed in confusion when he put down the clipboard, and her name was not called.

"The student I am about to call has topped the class because of her consistency, her dedication to her craft, and her artistry. These are attributes that make an excellent pastry chef, and today, Miss Parker, you have proven you have what it takes to be just that. Congratulations."

Amy's hand flew to her mouth in disbelief as her classmates clapped.

"That's not fair. The only reason she scored so high is that she has Gabriel wrapped around her finger. No wonder her cake looks so good. Must be nice to have connections," she heard Seline say loud enough for her classmates to hear.

Amy's expression hardened, her eyes narrowing at Seline's attempt to diminish her achievement. She crossed the room and stood before her. "Seline, my cake is the result of hard work and dedication, not any so-called connections. I earned this," she seethed.

Before Seline could respond, Professor Reynolds approached them. His voice carried authority as he addressed the brewing conflict. "Seline, I won't tolerate baseless accusations. Amy's talent and skill have earned her every accolade she receives. Besides, I personally scored her two percent higher than Gabriel."

The room fell silent, the weight of Professor Reynolds' words sinking in. Seline, defeated, retreated to her workstation, her face flushed with embarrassment.

Amy beamed, her heart brimming with pride and relief. She glanced at Gabriel, and a knowing smile passed between them.

"Congratulations!" Gabriel exclaimed; his voice filled with genuine admiration. "I'm not playing favorites, but I knew you would have come out on top." He grinned.

Amy's cheeks flushed with red as she basked in Gabriel's praise. "Thanks. I would hug you, but I don't want to give Seline more ammunition." She half chuckled, looking around.

"You deserve it. No matter what anyone else has to say," Gabriel said with a determined set of his jaw. Amy gave him a grateful smile. A flicker of unease shadowed her eyes.

"Hey, what's wrong?" Gabriel asked, his voice filled with genuine care. "You seem preoccupied."

Amy hesitated for a moment, contemplating whether to share her inner turmoil with him. But as she looked into his eyes, she found solace in his unwavering support. She took a deep breath, her voice quivering slightly. "I found out something today... about my biological father," she began, her words trailing off.

Gabriel's brows furrowed as he leaned closer, urging her to continue. "Did you find him?" he asked carefully.

Amy swallowed hard, her heart pounding in her chest. "He passed away," she confessed, her voice barely above a whisper. "But that's not all. He had another daughter. I have a half-sister. She's only sixteen. And his parents, my grandparents, are still alive too."

Gabriel's eyes widened with surprise, his hand still resting gently on her arm. "Wow, that's a lot to process," he said softly, his voice filled with empathy. "Have you thought about reaching out to them?"

Amy's face contorted with a mix of fear and uncertainty. "I... I don't know, Gabriel," she admitted. "They probably have no idea he had another child. I'm scared of how they'll react. What if they reject me?"

Gabriel's grip on her arm tightened, offering her a sense of grounding. His voice exuded unwavering support. "Amy, I understand your fears, but you deserve to have a connection with your family. They might be just as surprised as you are, but that doesn't mean they won't accept you. You won't know until you try."

Amy mulled over his words before glancing up into his eyes filled with concern. "You're right," she said, her lips quirking up in a small smile. "I'll do it after the holidays. Hopefully, by then, I'll have enough courage."

Gabriel smiled encouragingly. "I'm here for you."

"Thanks." She smiled gratefully. "So, are you coming

to the clam chowder cookoff?" she asked, changing the topic.

"I'll be there," he promised.

"Okay. I'll see you tomorrow. Bye, Gabriel."

"Bye, Amy." He smiled affectionately. As she pulled out of the parking lot, she glanced in the rearview mirror to see him standing there watching her car leave, and a smile broke out on her lips. After all the disappointment from the men in her life, it seemed she had found a good one after all.

The next day, the sun was out and bright, tempering the autumn chill. Amy raised her head, basking in the gentle heat from its rays. The air was thick with the tantalizing aroma of simmering spices and savory broths, beckoning Amy to draw closer to the heart of the event.

"Hey, Amy. Come try this," Nikki called out, catching her attention from a colorful tent on the other side.

"Wanna go try some?" She squinted up at Gabriel with an inviting smile.

"You go." He smiled back. "I'm gonna see if Paul needs any help in setting up his booth."

"Okay," she replied, applying a squeeze to their intertwined fingers before they unraveled from each other, and she walked away. "What have we got here?" she asked, a smile tugging at the corners of her lips.

"It's clam chowder," Nikki informed her. Amy accepted the spoon from her aunt and wrapped her lips around the utensil, pulling off the food.

"Oh, it's hot!" Amy exclaimed as the flavor erupted in her mouth.

"They don't call it a clam chowder competition for nothing," Nikki grinned, handing her a bottle of water.

"The flavor...it's unique. I like it. But I'm not sure I'll

last very long if everything here is that delicious," Amy advised.

"Do like me. Only taste a morsel from each station, and by the time you're finished, it will be a whole meal—you'll be fine," Nikki advised. Amy nodded in acceptance. "Let's go find the others."

The women made their way through the bustling tents, each one showcasing the culinary skills of the participants.

They spotted the rest of the group standing around Paul's booth. "Hey, Amy. Welcome to Clam Chowder Central!" he greeted them when they arrived. "I've got my secret recipe simmering away. You're in for a treat."

"Can't wait." Amy smiled.

"This one has a nice kick to it," Trish remarked, sipping from a small cup.

"What's that?" Amy inquired.

"It's a family secret." Trish held out the cup to her, and Amy took a small sip, savoring the flavor of the soup.

"You should try this too, Miss Murphy," Gabriel spoke, handing Trish another cup.

"Please, Gabriel, just call me Trish," she spoke with an encouraging smile.

"Okay...Trish. What do you think?" he asked, eyes filled with anticipation.

"Mmm. It's really nice. You really know how to pick them, Gabriel," Trish smiled encouragingly.

Amy watched as Trish and Gabriel engaged in animated conversation, their laughter mingling with the lively atmosphere around them. It warmed her heart to see the people she cared about getting along.

"Amy!" She turned to see Sarah and Aaron approaching.

"Hi, Sarah and Aaron." She hugged them in greeting. "How's my little Buttercup doing?"

"She's doing great," Sarah replied, rubbing her protruding belly. "We've had a few bumps here and there, but nothing serious."

"I'm glad to hear that because I can't wait to meet my little princess," Amy beamed.

As the day wore on, the group continued to have fun sharing in the festivities around them. The sun began its descent, casting a golden glow over the event. The crowd gathered around the main stage, where the winners of the cookoff would soon be announced. Excitement crackled in the air as the anticipation built.

"Third place goes to..."

"And the second place goes to..." boomed the announcer's voice, causing a hush to fall over the crowd.

"Paul!" The crowd erupted in applause and cheers as Paul stepped forward to accept his well-deserved recognition.

Amy's face beamed with pride as she nestled into the warmth of Gabriel's body, and he wrapped his arms around her waist from behind.

Chapter Twenty-Five

The grand ballroom of the local hotel was adorned with elegant decorations, twinkling lights, and floral centerpieces. The air was filled with excitement as guests mingled and chatted, dressed in their finest attire.

Trish glanced around, taking in the sight of the bustling room filled with supporters and animal lovers alike.

The time came for Trish to take the stage; her palms were slightly sweaty as she grasped the microphone. The room hushed, and all eyes turned to her. She took a deep breath, her voice steady as she began her speech.

"Ladies and gentlemen, thank you all for joining us tonight. We gather here not only to enjoy a delightful evening, but also to make a difference in the lives of our furry friends who rely on us for their well-being," Trish spoke passionately, her eyes scanning the crowd, searching for understanding and empathy.

"Animals are vulnerable beings, innocent and pure.

They bring us joy and unconditional love, asking for nothing in return. However, many of them suffer from neglect, abuse, and abandonment. It is our responsibility, as compassionate individuals, to extend our hands and hearts to these voiceless creatures."

Her voice resonated in the room, and a soft murmur of agreement and empathy rippled through the crowd. Trish continued, her words weaving a tapestry of hope and compassion.

"Tonight, we have gathered to raise funds to ensure that the Humane Society can continue its noble mission of rescuing, rehabilitating, and finding forever homes for these precious animals. With your generous contributions, we can make a tangible difference in their lives, providing them with the care and love they so desperately need."

As Trish concluded her speech, applause filled the room, and she made her way back to her seat, her heart still fluttering with a mix of emotions. She sat down next to Reed, who smiled at her warmly.

"You did an incredible job, Trish," Reed whispered, his voice filled with admiration. "Your words touched everyone's hearts. I'm so proud of you."

Trish blushed, grateful for Reed's kind words. "Thank you, Reed. I just hope that our message resonates with everyone. We have a long way to go, but together, we can make a real difference."

Reed nodded; his gaze filled with determination. "Absolutely, Trish. We have an amazing team of dedicated individuals here, and I'm confident that tonight's event will be a resounding success. We'll be able to provide better care for the animals and create a brighter future for them."

Trish smiled, her heart swelling with gratitude for the support she had in Reed and the entire committee. Together, they would continue their fight for the vulnerable animals, fueled by their shared passion and the belief that love and compassion could change lives.

Reed, sitting next to her, leaned in and whispered, "Trish, you were amazing up there. Your words touched everyone's hearts."

Trish blushed, grateful for Reed's kind words. She turned to face him, her eyes sparkling with gratitude. "Thank you, Reed. It means a lot to me. I just hope our message resonates with everyone here tonight."

"Ladies and gentlemen, may I have your attention," Kerry, one of the committee member's voice rang out from the podium. She was a charismatic woman with a commanding voice. "It is time for our auction!" she announced. "Tonight, we have an extraordinary opportunity for you to make a difference while enjoying an unforgettable evening. We have a special twist this year, as we'll be auctioning off dates with some of our most eligible bachelors and bachelorettes, who have been kind enough to volunteer themselves."

The crowd erupted into cheers and applause; their enthusiasm contagious. Trish glanced at the participants, catching glimpses of nervous smiles and excited whispers. She spotted Amy standing in the corner, her eyes shining with a mix of anticipation and nervousness. Her eyes tracked her daughter until their eyes connected.

"You've got this," she mouthed, giving her a thumbs-up. Amy smiled appreciatively and nodded.

As the bidding started, Amy was the first to step onto the stage. "Allow me to introduce the remarkable Amy, a twenty-one-year-old culinary arts student specializing in the art of pastries. For those with a sweet tooth, this one is especially for you."

The crowd rumbled with laughter at the presenter's fun jabs.

"Not only is she an undeniable talent, but she is also an avid nature enthusiast with a deep love for the great outdoors. Amy finds solace and inspiration in the embrace of nature's beauty. Whether she's traversing breathtaking landscapes on exhilarating hikes or immersing herself in the refreshing waters of lakes and rivers, she embraces the wonders of the natural world."

Trish's head bobbed as she looked on, impressed at the way Kerry was able to sell Amy. Even she was tempted to place a bid.

"The bidding will start at one hundred dollars. Do I hear one fifty?" Kerry asked, looking expectantly at the guests.

"One fifty," Gabriel proudly raised his paddle.

"Two hundred," another gentleman raised his almost immediately.

The back-and-forth went on until Gabriel bid a whopping one thousand dollars, much to the delight of the guests and Amy, whose eyes shined bright with affection as he helped her from the stage. Next, it was Nikki's turn, and in like fashion, Paul outbid the other guests. Trish was happy with how everything was turning out as each bid went over five hundred dollars.

"And now, for the moment you have all been waiting for. Ladies, get your checkbooks ready." Trish's eyes widened in surprise when Reed walked out onto the stage.

"The remarkable Mr. Reed Hastings, president of the

Humane Society..." Applause erupted, cutting Kerry's introduction. "Not only is he a philanthropist with a very big heart, but he epitomizes integrity and compassion. Not only does he generously contribute his time and resources to the Humane Society, but he is also deeply passionate about the cause. The well-being of our furry friends is dear to his heart, and he tirelessly works toward creating a better world for them." Trish's head automatically bobbed in agreement.

"Now..." Kerry's eyes glinted with mischief as a playful smirk graced her lips. "Let's talk about what makes Reed such an exceptional catch. Not only is he a dedicated advocate, but he is also a fine specimen of a man. With his charming smile, impeccable style, and magnetic presence, Reed undoubtedly turns heads wherever he goes. He is the embodiment of grace and sophistication. For this one, we will begin the bid at two hundred."

A woman in the back raised her paddle immediately, followed by another, then another. The bids escalated rapidly, and Trish's heart raced.

"Fifteen hundred." She raised her paddle. Reed's approving smile filled her with excitement.

"Two thousand." Trish turned her head to find Melissa behind her with her paddle raised and a competitive glare. There was no way Trish was losing Reed to that woman.

"Looks like Melissa's gunning for your guy," Nikki vocalized.

"Yeah, well, we'll see about that," Trish replied with a determined set of her jaw. "Two thousand five hundred." She raised her paddle.

"Three thousand five hundred." Trish swiveled in her seat to give the woman an 'Are you serious' look. Melissa simply angled her head in challenge, a smirk crossing her lips. There was no way she was losing to this woman.

"Five thousand." Trish raised her paddle again, waiting.

"Five thousand going once, going twice, sold to Trish Murphy. Didn't I tell you this was going to be an exciting one?" Kerry grinned.

Reed's eyes widened in surprise as he realized Trish had won. A mixture of relief and joy washed over his face. "Wow, that was intense," he said when he returned to their table.

Trish smiled, her heart swelling with affection. "You're worth it," she replied softly, her voice filled with sincerity.

At that moment, time seemed to stand still as Reed leaned in, his lips gently meeting hers. The world around them faded away, leaving only the warmth of their embrace and the overwhelming sense of connection.

"Get a room, you two."

They pulled apart then, Trish's cheeks reddening in embarrassment. She turned to see Amy and the others grinning. "You guys look so in love," Amy vocalized.

Trish turned to Reed, and their gazes locked. A newfound certainty filled her heart. "We are," she confirmed, her lips lifted in a soft smile.

As the function progressed deep into the night, Trish found herself alongside Reed, entertaining conversations with the guests as they tried to provide as much information on the Society as possible. As she weaved her way through the crowd, her eyes caught sight of a familiar figure tucked away in a dimly lit corner.

"Nelly, I'm so happy to see you," Trish greeted the older woman, planting a kiss on her cheek.

"Hi, dear. You know me. I love good dress-up parties as much as the next person." Nelly grinned, the laugh lines around her mouth and the crow's feet at the corners of her eyes prominent.

"You look lovely," Trish appraised, taking in the red chiffon dress she wore.

"Thank you, dear. You look quite lovely yourself," Nelly returned the compliment. Her eyes grew distant for a moment as if lost in memories. Then she nodded thoughtfully. "Trish, I was wondering if you could help me with something. I know you said you didn't want to hear anything about your father, but this is important. Do you happen to know if your parents had any other close relatives?"

Trish furrowed her brow, curious by the question. "Well, my mother had a sister who lives in Colorado—Aunt Connie. We're not particularly close, but we've spoken a few times. She has two daughters. As for my father, Stew, he was an only child. His mother passed away when he was a teenager, and his father died when Nikki and I were very young."

Nelly nodded, absorbing the information. "Interesting," she murmured. "And what about your father's properties? Did he ever own anything on Camano Island?"

Trish's eyes widened in surprise. "Camano Island? No, I don't think so. The house we used to stay in during the holidays was always a rental. Why do you ask?"

Nelly's gaze turned apologetic. "I'm sorry for prying, my dear, but I'm trying to confirm something. As soon as I am sure, I will let you know."

"Okay," Trish responded, her brows furrowed in

confusion. "Well, I guess I will be waiting. It was great seeing you, Nelly."

"You too, my dear," Nelly patted her arm. Trish walked off, not sure what to make of the conversation they'd just had.

When the event ended, Nikki and Amy ended up needing a ride, as Paul had to take Sarah home because Aaron had been paged to head back to the hospital. Gabriel followed him, needing to discuss something important.

"I've got a surprise for you," Trish declared, her voice filled with excitement as they approached Reed's car. She turned to Reed and extended her hand. "Can I have the keys?" Reed smiled encouragingly as he placed the keys in her hand.

Nikki and Amy exchanged bewildered glances, their brows furrowing in confusion. "Trish, are you sure about this?" Nikki asked, concern lacing her words.

Trish smiled, her eyes shining with determination. "I have been facing my fears head-on with Reed's help for a couple of weeks now. I'm ready for this," she replied, her voice steady and resolute.

Nikki and Amy rushed to Trish, enveloping her in a tight hug. Tears streamed down their faces, mingling with smiles of pride. "We're so proud of you, Mom," Amy whispered, her words choked with emotion.

Trish's heart swelled with gratitude and a newfound sense of empowerment, and she embraced her family tightly. She slid into the driver's seat. Reed settled beside her, offering a reassuring smile as the others settled in the back.

The engine roared to life, its sound filling the night

air, as Trish navigated the familiar streets with newfound determination. She drove with caution, and each turn and stop sign was a testament to her bravery as she drove her family home.

Epilogue

The sun had barely risen, casting a warm golden glow through the kitchen window.

Trish stood at the kitchen counter, her hands plunged deep into the cavity of the turkey, expertly stuffing it with a fragrant mixture of herbs and bread-crumbs. As she worked, her brow furrowed in concentration; she couldn't help but smile at the joyful chatter filling the room.

"There we were in the middle of the skating rink, flat on our butts, laughing while the other skaters looked at us like we'd gone mad," Amy chuckled, the melodious sound filling the kitchen.

Trish looked over at her daughter, a smile lifting her lips as she listened to her talk about Gabriel. She could tell Amy was already smitten with the young man, and from their conversations, it was evident Gabriel was enamored by her daughter as well. It eased the apprehensions she'd had at the beginning, and she was now genuinely happy Amy had found someone who made her happy.

"What happened after?" Nikki, standing at the other end of the counter, turned to ask.

"We spent the next five minutes trying to pick ourselves off the ice. In the end, we ended up crawling on our knees to the edge of the rink," Amy replied.

"How did you not learn to skate? It's like second nature to your mom and me." Nikki's brows furrowed.

Amy's eyes clouded before she lowered her head. "It's just one of those things I didn't get around to learning growing up with my adoptive parents," she spoke lightly, her eyes focused on the rolling pin as she vigorously rolled out the dough for the pie.

Trish's heart clenched at Amy's despondent expression. There was so much her daughter had missed growing up—so much she would have wanted to give her if she had been in her life back then. "I have an idea. Why don't we all go skating after the holidays?" she offered in a hopeful tone. "My leg's all better now. I could teach you a few tricks."

Amy looked up then, her blue eyes now alight with hope and appreciation. "I would like that very much," she responded with a smile.

Trish smiled, her chest filling with warmth. "That's the spirit," Nikki spoke up, breaking the tender moment that passed between them. "Our past experiences might not have been great, but I am so happy that we're all getting a second shot at creating wonderful memories together," she added with feeling.

"You're right. We are creating new memories— wonderful ones at that," Trish agreed, nodding.

The kitchen settled into a comfortable silence as the group continued working on getting everything ready for later.

"Nikki, how's that macaroni casserole coming along?" Trish asked, glancing over her shoulder.

Nikki, her curly hair gathered in a loose bun, stirred the bubbling pot on the stove. "It's coming along just fine. I added some extra cheese this time. You know, to make it extra cheesy and gooey. I hope that's okay."

Trish chuckled. "It's definitely going to be a hit if the smell from here is anything to go by. Plus, mac and cheese is always a crowd-pleaser."

"Right?" Nikki chuckled.

The doorbell rang then. "I'll get it," Amy offered, brushing off the thin dust of flour on her hands on her apron. She left the kitchen and, in less than a minute, came back with Reed, who held a bottle of wine in one hand and a pumpkin pie in the other. His eyes met Trish's, and a gentle smile formed on his lips. Trish's heart skipped a beat as she put the turkey aside and walked over to greet him.

"Hey, Reed," Nikki greeted.

"Hi, Nikki," he greeted back before adding, "It smells like heaven in here."

"Oh, we try our best," Nikki replied, a glint in her blue eyes. Reed chuckled before turning his attention to Trish, who was now standing before him.

"Hi," Reed greeted, leaning in for a kiss. Trish welcomed his embrace, their lips meeting in a tender moment of affection.

"What's that you've got there?" Trish asked, peering at the pumpkin pie.

Reed grinned. "I stopped by Ms. Anderson's bakery on my way over and couldn't resist. Thought it would make a perfect addition to our feast later."

Trish's eyes filled with admiration. "You're amazing. You know that?"

Reed's cheeks reddened slightly as he brushed a strand of hair away from Trish's face. "I want to be amazing for you." Trish's own cheeks reddened at his declaration.

"Are you staying?" Trish asked with a hopeful expression.

Reed's expression grew apologetic. "I'm sorry. I can't. I'm going to swing by the homeless shelter. I have a box of items to drop off for the local welfare committee. They're preparing a Thanksgiving meal for the people there."

Trish's eyes sparkled with pride. "That's incredibly thoughtful, Reed. You have such a kind heart."

"It's the right thing to do. How can we be thankful for all our blessings and not be willing to share with others who are not so fortunate?" he asked as Trish walked him to the front door.

"Have I told you how much I love you?" she asked with a twinkle in her eyes.

"A few times," Reed smiled. "But I will never get tired of hearing you say it though. I love you."

"And I will never get tired of hearing you say it either," Trish returned with an affectionate smile.

He gave her a quick peck on the lips before grabbing his coat. "I'll be back soon," he promised.

As Reed left, Trish returned to the kitchen, a sense of satisfaction and purpose filling her as she joined the lively conversation happening between her daughter and her sister. She carefully placed the stuffed turkey in the oven, and less than fifteen minutes later, the aromatic scent of roasting meat enveloped the kitchen. With a quick glance at the recipe, she began preparing the baste, a symphony of flavors coming together in a small bowl.

Five hours later, Trish stood in the center of the beautifully decorated dining room, her eyes glistening with a mixture of pride and joy. The long table was adorned with autumn-themed centerpieces, and the aroma of roasted turkey filled the air, mingling with the scent of freshly baked pies and cheesy mac and cheese.

"This is quite the spread," Nikki remarked. "I haven't had a Thanksgiving meal like this in quite some time."

"Me either," Trish confessed, her lips turning up in a satisfied smile at the work they had accomplished in preparing the meal for their newly formed family.

"You ladies truly outdid yourselves," Paul announced his presence behind them, planting a kiss on Nikki's cheek.

Nikki reached up and lovingly rested her hand against his cheek as his chin rested on her shoulder. "Hi, babe," she greeted with a sweet smile that transformed her expression.

"Hi, Paul," Trish smiled.

"I brought ham." He straightened up and revealed the succulent-looking smoked ham glistening from the glaze.

"This smells wonderful, Chef Thompson." Nikki smiled as she stared at him from under her lashes. Paul's eyes glinted with mischief and something else.

"All right, you two. Leave your hot moments until after the meal," Trish interrupted, taking the ham from Paul and placing it on the table.

Sarah and Aaron walked in just then with Amy behind them.

"Hi, Nikki, Trish," Sarah greeted.

"Hi, sweetheart." Nikki smiled wide, taking Sarah into her arms. She turned to Aaron and did the same.

"Hi, guys," Trish greeted.

"It smells great in here."

"Wait until you taste it," Nikki said confidently.

As they all moved to take their seats around the table, the doorbell rang. "I'll get it," Amy jumped up. When she returned, Reed was beside her. Trish's lips automatically shot up in a satisfied grin.

"I hope I'm not too late," he spoke.

"Not at all. We just sat down," Trish assured him. Relief passed over his face as he walked to the table and took the chair opposite Trish.

"Good. We're all here. Let's eat," Nikki announced.

The doorbell rang again. "I'll get it," Trish said, rising to her feet. When she opened the door, Kaylyn stood on the other side, holding a beautifully baked pie in her hands.

"I brought pie." Kaylyn smiled.

Trish's face lit up with a wide smile. "Kaylyn, you didn't have to bring anything."

Kaylyn chuckled, her eyes sparkling with mischief. "Oh, come on, Trish. It's Thanksgiving! I couldn't show up empty-handed. Besides, this pie is something special. My grandma's secret recipe."

Trish's heart swelled with affection for her friend. "Thank you. You're such a sweetheart."

"You're welcome," Kaylyn responded, giving her a warm hug. "I'm headed home now. I don't want to keep Ben and the girls waiting. He usually starts carving the turkey before four."

"Oh, that means you have to go now if you want to make that turkey curfew." Trish chuckled playfully.

Kaylyn played along with a chuckle of her own. "Bye, Trish. Happy Thanksgiving," she bade farewell.

"Bye, Kaylyn. Say hi to Ben and the girls for me." Trish smiled. Kaylyn gave a quick nod before descending the porch steps and heading to her car. Trish closed the door and headed back to the dining room.

"Look what Kaylyn dropped off," she announced as she walked through the door.

"Oh, more pie," Nikki grinned mischievously. "I'm guessing by the time we're done eating, none of us will be able to move from this table." The others chuckled.

Placing the pie on the table, Trish took her seat. "Let's pray," she said, holding her hands out to Nikki and Amy, who were on either side of her. Holding hands, the group bowed their heads. "Dear Lord, we give thanks for all you have provided and for your continued blessings. Please help us not to take for granted all that we have and remember those who have nothing and bless them. Amen."

"Amen," everyone responded in unison. They dug into the food then.

Trish took in the laughter and conversation that filled the air. Her eyes landed on Amy and Nikki as they laughed and shared with the others, and a warm feeling filled her chest. She had been hopeful for a day like this, but there had been doubts that it would ever happen. Now that it was a reality, she felt overjoyed. A tear slipped down her cheek.

"Trish, are you all right?" Paul's concerned voice interrupted her thoughts.

She turned to him with a reassuring smile. "I am."

"You're crying," he pointed out.

"Tears of joy." The table had grown silent as everyone

looked at her with concern. Feeling a surge of emotions, Trish stood, her voice filled with love and gratitude as she addressed her family. "Today, as we gather together, I am overwhelmed with joy. This past year has been a roller coaster, filled with uncertainties and pain. But it was also filled with love, strength, and hope. As I look at each and every one of you, I am overjoyed that I have been given a second chance, not only in life but in having a family. Here is to creating more wonderful memories together." She raised her glass, and the others followed suit, their faces sporting smiles of affection.

Paul rose from his seat then, a look of apprehension in his eyes. He cleared his throat, capturing everyone's attention. "I am really happy Trish started off the speeches so beautifully. I give it ten out of ten," he started, garnering chuckles from the others. "I want to create wonderful memories with the woman I loved and lost a long time ago, but by some stroke of luck, she is back in my life. I don't want to wait too long this time," he declared, his voice filled with determination and love. He knelt down on one knee, revealing a small velvet box in his hand. Gasps of surprise echoed through the room. Nikki's eyes widened in surprise as her hand covered her mouth.

"Nikki, my love," Paul continued, his voice trembling with emotion. "Will you marry me?"

The room held its breath for what seemed like forever before Nikki slowly nodded, then exclaimed, "Yes! Of course, I'll marry you."

The room erupted in applause as Paul slid the ring onto Trish's finger and pulled her into a loving embrace as they shared a tender kiss.

"Well done, Dad," Sarah beamed as Paul settled back into his chair.

"Thanks, kiddo," Paul chuckled. He turned and looked at Reed, a mischievous smirk on his lips. "I guess the impetus is on you now, buddy."

"Oh, believe me. I'm taking notes." Reed chuckled. Trish felt her cheeks redden as all eyes turned to her.

After the hearty Thanksgiving dinner, the group settled in the living room as Reed sat by the piano. Soft music filled the room as his fingers gracefully danced over the keys.

"Look! It's snowing!" Nikki excitedly pointed to the window.

The family's attention shifted to the window, where delicate snowflakes began to fall from the darkened sky. The room was filled with gasps and whispers of wonder. They gathered around, their faces pressed against the glass, watching as the snowflakes danced and twirled in the night.

As snowflakes settled on the ground, Trish felt a sense of peace settle within her. Surrounded by the warmth of her new and extended family, she knew she had finally achieved all her heart had ever hoped for. And as the snow continued to fall, they stood together, their hearts connected, embracing the joy and magic of the holiday season.

Coming Next

Pre Order Anchored in Hope

·

Other Books by Kimberly

The Archer Inn

An Oak Harbor Series

A Yuletide Creek Series

A Festive Christmas Series

A Cape Cod Series

Echoes of Camano Series

Connect with Kimberly Thomas

Amazon
Facebook
Newsletter
BookBub

To receive exclusive updates from Kimberly, please sign
up to be on her Newsletter!

CLICK HERE TO SUBSCRIBE

Made in the USA
Middletown, DE
16 March 2025

72763122R00133